Máiread Corrigan and Betty Williams

Women Changing the World

Aung San Suu Kyi
Standing Up for Democracy in Burma

Rigoberta Menchú
Defending Human Rights in Guatemala

Máiread Corrigan and Betty Williams
Making Peace in Northern Ireland

Máiread Corrigan and Betty Williams

Making Peace in Northern Ireland

Sarah Buscher and Bettina Ling

The Feminist Press
at The City University of New York
New York

Published by The Feminist Press at The City University of New York
City College, Wingate Hall, Convent Avenue at 138th Street, New York, NY 10031

First edition, 1999

Library of Congress Cataloging-in-Publication Data

Buscher, Sarah.
    Mairead Corrigan and Betty Williams: making peace in Northern Ireland /
Sarah Buscher and Bettina Ling. — 1st ed.
        p.   cm. — (Women changing the world)
    Summary: A joint biography of two women whose personal experiences with the killings in Northern Ireland led them to form the Peace People and work tirelessly to end the violence that has long plagued this country.
    ISBN 1-55861-200-9 (lib. bdg.).—ISBN 1-55861-201-7 (pbk.)
    1. Northern Ireland—History—1969–1994—Juvenile literature. 2. Peace movements—Northern Ireland—History—20th century—Juvenile literature. 3. Women and peace—Northern Ireland—History—20th century—Juvenile literature. 4. Peace Movement in Northern Ireland —Juvenile literature. 5. Corrigan, Mairead—Juvenile literature. 6.Williams, Betty—Juvenile literature. [1. Corrigan, Mairead. 2. Williams, Betty. 3. Northern Ireland—History—1969–1994. 4. Peace movements—Northern Ireland. 5. Pacifists. 6. Women—Biography.]
I. Ling, Bettina. II. Title. III. Series.
DA990.U46B857 1999
941.60824—dc21   98-44172
                                                                                                              CIP
                                                                                                              AC

The Feminist Press is grateful to the Ford Foundation for their generous support of our work. The Feminist Press is also grateful to Johnetta B. Cole, William L. Hedges, Florence Howe, Joanne Markell, Caroline Urvater, Genevieve Vaughan, Susan Weiler and Lynn Gernert, and Patricia Wentworth and Mark Fagan for their generosity in supporting this publication.

Printed on acid-free paper by RR Donnelley & Sons

Manufactured in Mexico

05   04   03   02   01   00   99   5   4   3   2   1

CONTENTS

WHAT DOES IT TAKE TO CHANGE THE WORLD?

Maybe this question sounds overwhelming. However, people who become leaders have all had to ask themselves this question at some point. They started finding answers by choosing how they would lead their lives every day and by creating their own opportunities to make a difference in the world. The anthropologist Margaret Mead said, "Never doubt that a small group of thoughtful, committed citizens can change the world; indeed it's the only thing that ever has." So let's look at some of the qualities possessed by people who are determined to change the world.

First, it takes vision. The great stateswoman and humanitarian Eleanor Roosevelt said, "You must do the thing you think you cannot do." People who change the world have the ability to see what is wrong in their society. They also have the ability to imagine something new and better. They do not accept the way things *are*—the "status quo"— as the only way things *must be* or *can be*. It is this vision of an improved world that inspires others to join leaders in their efforts to make change. Leaders are not afraid to be different, and the fear of failure does not prevent them from trying to create a better world.

Second, it takes courage. Mary Frances Berry, former head of the U.S. Commission on Civil Rights, said, "The time when you need to do something is when no one else is willing to do it, when people are saying it can't be done." People who change the world know that courage means more than just saying what needs to be changed. It means deciding to be active in the effort to bring about change—no matter what it takes. They know they face numerous challenges: they may be criticized, made fun of, ignored, alienated from their friends and family, imprisoned, or even killed. But even though they may sometimes feel scared, they continue to pursue their vision of a better world.

Third, it takes dedication and patience. The Nobel Prize–winning scientist Marie Curie said, "One never notices what has been done; one can only see what remains to be done." People who change the world understand that change does not happen overnight. Changing the world is an ongoing process. They also know that while what they do is important, change depends on what others do as well. Their original vision may transform and evolve over time as it interacts with the visions of others and as circumstances change. And they know that the job is never finished. Each success brings a new challenge, and each failure yet another obstacle to overcome.

Finally, it takes inspiration. People who change the world find strength in the experiences and accomplishments of others who came before them. Sometimes these role models are family members or personal friends. Sometimes they are great women and men who have spoken out and written about their own struggles to change the world for the better. Reading books about these people—learning about their lives and reading their own words— can be a source of inspiration for future world-changers. For example, when I was young, someone gave me a book called *Girls' Stories of Great Women,* which provided me with ideas of what women had achieved in ways I had never dreamed of and in places that were very distant from my small town. It helped me to imagine what I could do with my life and to know that I myself could begin working toward my goals.

This series of books introduces us to women who have changed the world through their vision, courage, determination, and patience. Their stories reveal their struggles as world-changers against obstacles such as poverty, discrimination, violence, and injustice. Their stories also tell of their struggles as women to overcome the belief, which still exists in most societies, that girls are less capable than boys of achieving high goals, and that women are less likely than men to become leaders. These world-changing women often needed even more vision and courage than their male counterparts, because as women they faced greater discrimination and resistance. They certainly needed more determination and patience, because no matter how much they proved themselves, there were always people who were reluctant to take their leadership and their achievements seriously, simply because they were women.

These women and many others like them did not allow these challenges to stop them. As they fought on, they found inspiration in women as well as men—their own mothers and grandmothers, and the great women who had come before them. And now they themselves stand as an inspiration to young women and men all over the world.

The women whose lives are described in this series come from different countries around the world and represent a variety of cultures. Their stories offer insights into the lives of people in varying circumstances. In some ways, their lives may seem very different from the lives of most people in the United States. We can learn from these differences as well as from the things we have in common. Women often share similar problems and concerns about issues such as violence in their lives and in the world, or the kind of environment we are creating for the future. Further, the qualities that enable women to become leaders, and to make positive changes, are often the same worldwide.

The first set of books in this series tells the stories of four women who have won what might be called humanity's highest honor: the Nobel Peace Prize.

The Nobel Peace Prize recognizes leaders who try to improve their societies using peaceful means. These leaders have faced many different kinds of challenges and have responded to them in different ways. But one goal they all share is to promote "human rights"—the basic rights to which all human beings are entitled.

In 1948, the United Nations adopted the *Universal Declaration of Human Rights,* which outlines the rights of all people to freedom from slavery and torture, and to freedom of movement, speech, religion, and assembly, as well as rights of all people to social security, work, health, housing, education, culture, and citizenship. Further, it states that all people have the equal right to all these human rights, "without distinction of any kind such as race, color, sex, language . . . or other status."

In the United States, many of these ideas are not new to us. Some of them can be found in the first ten amendments to the U.S. Constitution, known as the Bill of Rights. Yet these ideals continually face many challenges, and they must be defended and expanded by every generation. They have been tested in this country, for example, by the Civil Rights Movement to end racial discrimination and the movement to bring about equal rights for women. They continue to be tested even today by various individuals and groups who are fighting for greater equality and justice.

All over the world, women and men work for and defend the common goal of human rights for all. In some places these rights are severely violated.

Tradition and prejudice as well as social, economic, and political interests often exclude women, in particular, from benefiting from these basic rights. Over the past decade, women around the world have been questioning why "women's rights" and women's lives have been deemed secondary to "human rights" and the lives of men. As a result, an international women's human rights movement has emerged, with support from organizations such as the Center for Women's Global Leadership, to challenge limited ideas about human rights and to alert all nations that "women's rights are human rights."

The following biography is the true story of women overcoming incredible obstacles—economic hardship, religious persecution, political oppression, and even the threat of violence and death—in order to peacefully achieve greater respect for human rights in their country. I am sure that you will find their story inspiring. I hope it also encourages you to join in the struggle to demand an end to all human rights violations—regardless of sex, race, class, or culture—throughout the world. And perhaps it will motivate you to become someone who just might change the world.

Charlotte Bunch
Founder and Executive Director
Center for Women's Global Leadership
Rutgers University

You can help to change the world now by establishing goals for yourself personally and by setting an example in how you live and work within your own family and community. You can speak out against unfairness and prejudice whenever you see it or hear it expressed by those around you. You can join an organization that is fighting for something you believe in, volunteer locally, or even start your own group in your school or neighborhood so that other people who share your beliefs can join you. Don't let anything or anyone limit your vision. Make your voice heard with confidence, strength, and dedication . . . and start changing the world today.

It means, once in a lifetime
That justice can rise up,
And hope and history rhyme.

—Seamus Heaney, *The Cure at Troy*

Betty Williams (left) and Máiread Corrigan (right), Northern Irish peace activists and Nobel Peace Prize winners in 1976.

Chapter 1
"WE SHALL OVERCOME . . ."

As Betty Williams and Máiread Corrigan joined the crowds gathering in Belfast on a rainy Saturday in October 1976, they knew they were in great danger. They had received several death threats from people who wanted them to stop the work they were doing. But the two women refused to be intimidated. For seven years, their homeland of Northern Ireland had been torn by violence, causing the loss of hundreds of innocent lives. Now Betty and Máiread were demanding an end to this violence.

They were not alone. Thousands of people had joined them to march up the Falls Road, through an area dominated by one of the groups responsible for the violence. Their destination was Falls Park, where they planned to hold a peace rally. Many of the marchers were nervous. They knew that participating in this march was dangerous, but Betty and Máiread's determination gave them courage.

The Falls Road is a bleak and threatening place. As Betty and Máiread led the marchers down the road, they passed litter-strewn, empty lots, crumbling houses, and the boarded-up shells of shops destroyed by bombs and government neglect. In some places a tattered, faded Irish flag, illegal in Northern Ireland, flew from a street lamp.

Through the rain, they could see that the gates of Falls Park were blocked by a crowd of angry teenagers. The teenagers began throwing rocks, bottles, and bricks at the demonstrators. A group of young women attacked the marchers—pulling hair, kicking, and striking people with umbrellas. Bloodied and bruised, with only their umbrellas to shield themselves, the marchers refused to fight back. These peaceful demonstrators wanted to show that violent attacks could not drive them to use violence in return. But they also refused to turn back. They wanted to show that they were not afraid to march anywhere—even on the Falls Road.

Because the gates of Falls Park had been locked, Máiread and Betty quickly decided to change the location of their meeting to Musgrave Park, about a mile away. The march went on, followed by a group that continued to shout abuse. The marchers were soaked and blood was visible on many faces, but no one abandoned the demonstration.

The marchers poured into Musgrave Park where they held a simple service. Everyone joined in singing hymns and praying for peace. Máiread and Betty briefly addressed the crowd, then stood aside for the next speaker. The marchers were stunned when they realized who she was.

Máiread's sister, Anne Maguire, had come to this rally in a wheelchair. She had a smashed pelvis and two broken legs. She stood in front of the crowd, supported by Máiread and some friends. Her presence on this day was very special. Anne was one of thousands of victims of the violence in Northern Ireland, and it was her experience that had inspired Betty and Máiread to take a stand for peace. In spite of her pain and grief, Anne knew she needed to be here today. She had an important message to share with the marchers. When she spoke, she spoke for all of them.

“We have a simple message for the world . . .” she declared. “We want to live and love and build a just and peaceful society. We want for our children, as we want for ourselves, our lives at home, at work and at play, to be lives of joy and peace.”

These desires seemed simple enough, but in Belfast, Northern Ireland, many had given up hope of ever achieving them. Peace seemed thousands of miles away—until now.

Since 1969, a war has been raging in Northern Ireland—an area of land about the size of Connecticut in the northern part of Ireland—over the future of the state. Northern Ireland remained part of the United Kingdom, which includes England, Scotland, and Wales, when the rest of Ireland became independent. The State of Northern Ireland is divided between Nationalists and Unionists. Nationalists want to use political means to get the British out of Northern Ireland and unite the state with the Republic of Ireland. Unionists want the state to remain part of the United Kingdom. More radical groups are the Republicans and Loyalists. Republicans share the same goal as Nationalists but support the use of violence to achieve their goals. Loyalists share the same goal as Unionists, but they, too support violence. The Irish Republican Army (IRA), a paramilitary organization (an armed force that is independent of the military), is a Republican group. Loyalist paramilitary forces include the Ulster Volunteer Force (UVF), the Ulster Defense Association (UDA), and the Ulster Freedom Fighters (UFF). Of course, the paramilitary groups would like to achieve their goals using political means, but they do not have confidence in political solutions. Each side feels betrayed by politicians.

These paramilitary groups, while small in number, have wreaked havoc throughout the country as they set off bombs, torch people's homes, hijack cars and buses, and kill or maim people. On the surface this looks like a sectarian, or religious, war because most Republicans are Catholic, and are angry at the repression of Catholics in Northern Ireland. Most Loyalists are Protestant, and want to hold on to the privileges many Protestants have gained by supporting the ruling powers in the United Kingdom. For Republican and Loyalist extremists, identifying one's religion is a way of identifying a friend or an enemy. However, in reality the conflict is less about religion than about political and economic power.

Thousands of innocent people have been killed or wounded by the actions of these violent extremists. Among these thousands were Anne Maguire and three of her children. A few months before the Falls Road march, they were hit by a car driven by a member of the IRA who was shot dead as he fled British soldiers. The three children were killed, and Anne was permanently injured.

Máiread Corrigan and Betty Williams had long been upset by the violence that surrounded them. But it was this tragedy that brought them together and made them resolve to do something about it. With the help of a journalist named Ciaran McKeown, they organized a group called the Peace People, and launched a peace movement in Northern Ireland. The movement organized some of the largest peace demonstrations in the history of Northern Ireland and even spread to the rest of the United Kingdom.

These demonstrations were attended by thousands of people from all over the world. The Peace People also worked in the cities and rural communities to try to bridge the divide between Catholics and Protestants.

As news of the movement spread, the Peace People won recognition and supporters worldwide. In October 1977, Máiread Corrigan and Betty Williams were jointly awarded the Nobel Peace Prize for their efforts to end the violence in Northern Ireland.

To most people, Betty and Máiread seemed like "ordinary" women. They both came from poor families in the working-class section of Belfast, and neither of them attended college. They grew up at a time when there was not a great deal of opportunity for women in Northern Ireland. Yet these two ordinary women found the inner strength to start a peace movement—originally made up mostly of women—that spread throughout Northern Ireland and reached into Europe and the United States. These two ordinary women won humanity's highest honor, and the attention of the world.

The peace movement did not permanently end the violence in Northern Ireland. Yet, in 1976 Máiread and Betty helped give the people of Northern Ireland the means to express their frustration with the violence and fear that had gripped their country for the previous eight years. They tapped into their country's longing for peace and gave people hope for a better future. They remain a timeless example of what the most ordinary of people can accomplish when they refuse to be governed by fear.

Chapter 2

THE HISTORY OF THE CONFLICT

Betty and Máiread's goal to bring peace to Northern Ireland was very courageous and ambitious. They were confronting hostilities that had lasted for centuries and prejudices that had been passed from one generation to the next by both Protestants and Catholics.

The troubled relationship between England and Ireland began when England made Ireland its colony. Under colonialism, a powerful foreign country controls the resources, the economy, and the government of the colonized country. As a result, the native inhabitants have little say in the control of their own country. It is the colonists—the foreigners—who usually benefit from this arrangement. For example, Ireland's resources, like agricultural products and timber, were exploited by England for economic gain.

Another characteristic of colonialism is to replace cultural traditions, such as language and religion, with those of the controlling country. The English colonists did this to the Irish natives. They imposed their own "civilized" language on the Irish. The English colonists also established a parliament—a type of governing body—based on the parliament model in England. This government was completely dominated by the English and did not represent the Irish. Ireland was comparable to the American colonies, which were originally controlled by England prior to winning freedom in the Revolutionary War.

The English also imposed their religion, which, at the time, was Catholicism, on the Irish natives. But this changed in 1534 when the English king, Henry VIII, established the Protestant Church of England and England became a Protestant country. As in the past, the English colonizers expected the Irish to follow their example and become Protestant, but the Irish remained Catholic.

The English government used a variety of means to repress the Irish. They took their land and gave it to Protestant Scottish colonists who were loyal to the king of England. These settlers were concentrated in an area in the north of Ireland called Ulster and came to be known as "Ulster Scots." This practice established a Protestant minority in the Catholic country. Although the Protestants were a minority, they had the support of England. As a result, they controlled Ireland politically and economically.

They also passed a series of laws, called Penal Laws, that denied Catholics—the majority of native Irish—their civil rights. Catholics were not allowed to educate their children, buy land, vote, bear arms, or hold jobs in the military, law, or politics. These laws reduced Catholics to second-class citizens with little economic or political power, and they increased the power of the Protestants. But not all Protestants supported the English government. In fact, in May of 1798, an organization called the United Irishmen led one of the largest rebellions in Irish history. They were headed by a Protestant lawyer named Theobald Wolfe Tone. He, like some other Protestant colonists, wanted Ireland to be an independent country. The fighting lasted for three months. Approximately 30,000 lives were lost. The rebellion was not suc-

What are some facts about Northern Ireland?

Northern Ireland covers an area of only 5,452 square miles, about the size of the state of Connecticut. It occupies the northeastern part of the island of Ireland.

Northern Ireland is shaped like a saucer, with highlands on the rim, lowlands in the center, and three mountain ranges: the Sperrin Mountains, the Antrim Mountains, and the Mourne Mountains. The population of Northern Ireland is approximately 1,631,800 people.

More than two-thirds of the land is used for agriculture, and most farms are owned by families. Much of the land is used for producing food for livestock. Barley and potatoes are planted on most of the remaining farmland. Flax, once an important crop, is now imported for the linen industry.

In Belfast, three important industries developed during the 1800s: linen weaving, rope-making, and shipbuilding. Extensive shipyards lie along Belfast Lough, northeast of the city. In fact, the *Titanic* was built here.

The population of Northern Ireland is divided by religion. According to the 1991 census, about 50 percent of the population are Protestants, 38.4 percent are Roman Catholics, and 11 percent indicate no religious affiliation. In general, the northeastern part of the state is predominantly Protestant, and the areas bordering the Republic of Ireland are primarily Roman Catholic.

The State of Northern Ireland is part of the United Kingdom, which is made up of England, Scotland, and Wales (Great Britain). These countries recognize the authority of the English monarch.

cessful. It only resulted in the English government tightening its control.

The Act of Union of 1800 dissolved the Irish Parliament. The English and Irish Parliaments were united in London. Irish Members of Parliament would now have to travel to London to represent their districts.

In 1845 to the mid-1850s, Ireland was completely transformed by the Potato Famine, also known as the Great Hunger (*An Gorta Mor* in Irish), a catastrophic event in Irish history. The Potato Famine was caused by the successive failures of the potato crop due to fungal infection. Farmers in Ireland had become dependent on the potato because it was cheap and easy to grow. When the crops failed, they began to starve. The famine claimed 1 million lives. Another 2 million people left Ireland and emigrated to the United States, Canada, England, and Australia. The English government did not give enough help to the Irish; relief efforts were delayed and poorly carried out. Some English politicians thought the English government should not help the Irish at all. They saw the famine as a way to get rid of the poor Irish people.

The division originally created by colonialism continued to grow. Political groups formed—some supporting the Act of Union, others opposing it in favor of "home rule." Home rule means the Irish would govern themselves and the English would no longer control them. Unionists, people supporting the Act of Union, feared the increasing popularity of the home rule movement. If the Irish gained home rule, then the wealthy, Protestant minority would lose its foothold in the government. Tensions mounted.

In 1905, a Nationalist party named Sinn Féin (Irish for "We ourselves") was founded. The Nationalists were influenced by the home rule movement and wanted Ireland to be independent of the United Kingdom.

Meanwhile, the Unionists continued to organize. In Ulster, where the Protestant minority was located, they vowed that if home rule was enacted, they would establish their own independent government in the north. But if the English government refused to grant Ireland home rule, they would remain loyal to England. The Ulster Volunteer Force (UVF), a Protestant paramilitary organization, was founded in 1913 to "defend" Ulster from home rule. In response, a group of radical Nationalists formed their own paramilitary organization to fight for independence—the Irish Volunteers. Guns had been brought into Irish politics.

In another attempt to gain home rule, the Irish Volunteers stormed and took over the General Post Office in Dublin on Easter Monday, April 24, 1916. This became known as the Easter Rising. Once again, the English government had the upper hand. The rebels were powerless against the military of the United Kingdom, and were swiftly defeated.

After the rebellion the English government imposed martial law. This means the military forces enforce the law. The leaders of the Rising were treated as traitors and fifteen of them were executed without a trial. The British also conducted massive sweeps of all Nationalist organizations and sent their members to jail.

After the Rising, Sinn Féin had two aims: to gain recognition of the Irish Republic and to allow the Irish people to choose their own form of government. The Irish Volunteers renamed themselves the Irish Army of the Republic, later to be called the Irish Republican Army (IRA). The IRA would serve as the military arm of Sinn Féin.

Elections were held in 1918 and Sinn Féin won massive support. The newly elected representatives created a separate government for Ireland. Meanwhile the IRA began an armed campaign to force the British out of Ireland. They attacked representatives of the British government, including politicians, soldiers, and the police.

As the IRA's armed campaign continued, the British took extra steps to stamp out Republican activity. They sent an additional force to retaliate against the IRA. They were called the "Black and Tans" for the uniform they wore. They were well-armed, undisciplined, and deadly. They waged a campaign of counter-terror, shooting suspected leaders of the IRA and many innocent Catholics as well. The Anglo-Irish war was underway.

In 1920, England established two home rule governments. One was in the north, in Ulster, and one in the South. That same year, the English also established a special police force for Ulster to aid in the war against the IRA. No attempt was made to enlist Catholics in this force. Again, England was giving control and power to the Protestants.

The Anglo-Irish war ended when England and Ireland signed a treaty in 1921 which established the Irish Free State in the South. Under the treaty, the new state of Ireland could govern itself while it

St. Eugene's Roman Catholic Cathedral in Derry dates back to 1873.

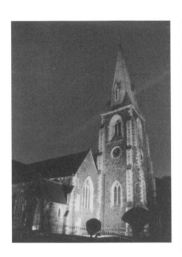

Saint Swithan's Parish Church in Derry is a part of the Presbyterian church, the largest Protestant denomination in Northern Ireland.

would still remain part of the Commonwealth—a group of countries that recognized the authority of the king or queen of England.

As expected, the government in Northern Ireland, still controlled by the Protestant minority, chose to remain allied with England. As a result, the island had been officially partitioned into two separate states.

The state of Northern Ireland was flawed from the beginning. It was born out of the Protestant Unionists' fear of Britain pulling out of Ireland. This would leave them a minority on an island dominated by Catholics. They feared they would experience the loss of political and economic power suffered by minorities: the loss of jobs, property, and political representation. There is a historical basis to this fear; it is the same discrimination that the Catholics in Ireland had suffered over the past four centuries.

Therefore, it was imperative to the Unionists that they retain political power. They accomplished this by denying Catholics economic and political power. They discriminated against Catholics in housing, jobs, voting, and even the right to a fair trial. The Special Powers Act, passed in 1922, gave the Royal Ulster Constabulary (RUC), Northern Ireland's police force, the power to arrest and detain suspects without trial for an indefinite period of time. It also allowed the RUC to use corporal punishment—physical punishment—which was used almost exclusively against Catholics as another means of repression. The Catholics in Northern Ireland were being denied their civil rights, which are rights granted to all citizens. These rights include equal treatment under the law, freedom from cruel and unusual punishment and discrimination, and the right to a speedy trial by jury. They also include freedom of religion and speech.

Many Catholics still hoped for a united Ireland that would one day be independent of England, but as time passed many Catholics worried less about a united Ireland and more about an issue that affected their every day lives—equal rights. More and more they began to speak out against the discrimination they suffered.

The late 1960s were a time of protest throughout the world, with a major civil rights movement growing in the United States. Following these examples, students in Northern Ireland began forming their own civil rights organizations. Protests demanding equal treatment of Catholics ended in violence when the activists were attacked by the RUC and Loyalists. Finally, the English government demanded that the Northern Irish government make reforms to end the discrimination against Catholics. While this appeased most of the civil rights organizations, the more radical groups were not satisfied. These groups continued to protest and the movement became more confrontational, resulting in more violence.

The lower-income areas where Republican and Loyalist extremists (the Catholic and Protestants who supported violence to achieve their goals) were concentrated were the areas of the most violence. Lower-income Catholics suffered the most from the discrimination of the Unionist government. Lower-income Protestants felt the most threatened by Catholics' demands for better jobs, fearing that they would lose their own jobs as a result. In fact, one Belfast resident told *Commonweal* magazine that the conflict was, "a fight between the have-nots on both sides."

Is there a connection between the civil rights movements in the United States and Northern Ireland?

The discrimination against Catholics in Northern Ireland was in many ways similar to the discrimination against African Americans in the United States. In both countries it was evident in employment, housing, and voting. In the United States segregation forced African Americans to go to different—often inferior—schools, sit in the back of buses, and use separate public facilities, like rest rooms and water fountains.

Although the U.S. Supreme Court found segregation unconstitutional in 1954, it was still practiced throughout the southern states. The civil rights movement was launched a year later with the Montgomery Bus Boycott—African Americans refused to ride the buses. This year-long boycott ended segregation on the buses of Montgomery, Alabama. From the boycott a young minister emerged as leader of the civil rights movement. His name was Martin Luther King, Jr.

Dr. King encouraged nonviolent protests, like sit-ins and marches, to bring about an end to discrimination. Civil rights activists organized campaigns, called protests, to give African Americans greater political power. Very often these protests were met with violence. Black churches were set on fire and some were bombed during services. Many civil rights activists, both black and white, were beaten, and some even murdered. Local police forces offered little protection; they often participated in the violence against the peaceful unarmed demonstrators.

After years of struggle, the 1964 Civil Rights Act declared that discrimination in voter registration, public facilities, and accommodations, like restaurants and hotels, and in hiring was illegal. It also denied federal funding to educational programs or institutions that practiced racial discrimination. It was a huge success for the civil rights movement, but there was still more work to be done.

A march across Alabama, from Selma to Montgomery, was organized in 1965 to protest discrimination in Alabama. Once again the protesters were attacked.

The civil rights movement in Northern Ireland drew inspiration from the U.S. movement and followed its example in organizing peaceful demonstrations. In January 1969, Northern Irish civil rights activists organized a Belfast–Derry march modeled after the Selma–Montgomery march. The route led them through miles of Unionist territory. This march was received with as much hostility as the march in Alabama. When the marchers reached the town of Burntollet they were ambushed by angry Loyalists who attacked them with rocks and broken bottles. When some of the marchers tried to leave the road and escape through the fields, the Royal Ulster Constabulary (RUC), the Northern Irish police force, beat them back. Dozens were injured and one woman was knocked unconscious.

Because of the violence the Unionist government took steps that seemed to discriminate against the Catholics, including imposing a curfew on the lower Falls Road (a Catholic area), completing house-to-house searches for weapons, wrecking and looting the homes of Catholics regardless of whether or not they were known to be involved with the IRA, and ultimately imposing internment. This measure consisted of arresting and holding people in jail indefinitely without a trial. In their first sweep the British army and RUC arrested 342 men suspected of IRA activity and brought them to holding centers for questioning.

Internment was completely one-sided. It only attempted to crush the IRA, not the Loyalist paramilitaries such as the UVF. It was also a major failure. The British did not have enough information about the IRA and as a result innocent men were arrested while the real IRA leaders walked free. However, internment was very effective in convincing many Catholics that the IRA was the only organization interested in protecting Catholics.

The arrests of IRA suspects continued and Catholics began to hear about the British army's use of a practice called "in-depth interrogation," a method of torture used on many suspects. Victims were beaten with batons, deprived of food and drink, forced to run over broken glass, and some were burned with cigarettes.

These abuses were a clear violation of basic human rights, and civil rights groups launched new protests demanding an end to internment. Again these protests were met with violence, and on January 30, 1972, the British army fired on unarmed civil rights demonstrators in Derry, killing thirteen and injuring thirteen. The day is now remembered as "Bloody Sunday."

After three years of horrible violence, the English government was convinced that the current government of Northern Ireland had no control of the situation and they decided to take direct control of this embattled state. The government of Northern Ireland was dissolved in March 1972 and once again the colony was directly controlled by the English government.

Four months later the IRA detonated twenty bombs throughout Belfast in just sixty-five minutes. At a shopping center where one of the blasts occurred, it seemed that the streets were covered with shattered glass, blood, and the bodies of the dead and injured. Nine people were killed and 130

What was "Bloody Sunday"?

On January 30, 1972, despite a government ban on marching, 15,000 people marched in Derry to protest internment. As the march began to disperse, returning to the Catholic section, the Bogside, the army began to arrest some of the marchers for defying the ban. Someone fired a gun, whether it was a soldier or a civilian has never been determined, but suddenly the British army lost control, firing into the crowd and shooting unarmed people in the back as they tried to flee. Thirteen men, seven of them under nineteen years of age, were killed and thirteen were injured. The day is now remembered as "Bloody Sunday."

The next day protests of these killings spread throughout Northern Ireland and Ireland. In Dublin 30,000 people marched to the British Embassy and burned it down. The killings remain a sensitive issue in British-Irish relations to this day. Many Catholics in Northern Ireland believe that the attack was planned in advance and they continue to demand that the British government reinvestigate the circumstances surrounding the killings. To them the day remains another painful reminder of British oppression.

people, both Catholics and Protestants, were injured in the blasts. But the violence was not over; three large bombs were detonated later that day in Derry. By midnight there were a total of thirty-nine explosions in Northern Ireland, bringing "Bloody Friday" to a close. When would this embattled country know peace?

The Bloody Sunday Monument in Derry is a reminder of the violence unarmed civil rights demonstrators faced on January 30, 1972, when the British army fired into the group killing thirteen people and injuring thirteen others.

Chapter 3

MÁIREAD CORRIGAN: CHOOSING PEACE

Máiread (pronounced mu-RADE—it is Irish for Margaret) Corrigan was born on January 27, 1944, in Belfast, the capital city of Northern Ireland. She was the second child in a family of five girls and two boys. The Corrigans lived in a small house in the Falls Road section of West Belfast, one of the most well known of the Catholic low-income areas in Belfast. Máiread's father was a windowwasher and her mother, a homemaker.

Máiread's parents both had a great influence on her. Máiread learned from her father that all people were equal and should be treated with respect and kindness. Her mother had a strong religious faith and a deep commitment to prayer and to the service of others. These qualities inspired Máiread to assist those in need and provided her with emotional and spiritual support in her work toward nonviolence.

Máiread was a happy, outgoing child with dark hair and green eyes. They were not a wealthy family, but they were a very close family. Máiread was especially close to her sister Anne, who was two years younger. Máiread attended Catholic schools, which was not unusual. In Northern Ireland the schools are almost completely segregated between Protestants and Catholics. Protestant children attend the state schools, while Catholic children attend private Catholic schools. The state schools are required by law to teach the Protestant religion. When this law

The Corrigan family. Andrew Corrigan (father), Margaret Corrigan (mother), Michael (Drew) Corrigan (brother), front row from left, Eilish Corrigan (sister), Anne Corrigan (sister), and Máiread Corrigan.

was enacted, the Catholic clergy became very angry and established their own schools, in which the Catholic religion would be taught.

Protestant and Catholic children were separated in other ways as well. For example, Catholics play Gaelic football and hurling—a game like field hockey. Protestants play cricket and rugby. Both Catholics and Protestants play football—what we call "soccer" in the United States—but the clubs they belong to or the team they support follows the religious divide.

Overall, children from Catholic and Protestant working-class backgrounds have very little contact with one another. This means they have little opportunity to form friendships that would help them overcome their dislike and distrust. These attitudes are reinforced at home, where parents tend to believe cultural stereotypes about the other group. All of this creates an "us versus them" outlook between working-class Protestants and Catholics. It is a vicious cycle. People learn prejudice from

Children play football, or "soccer" as it is called in the United States, in front of British army armored personnel carriers.

their parents and pass it on to their children, who pass it on to their children.

Despite being Catholic, Máiread did not feel especially loyal to the Nationalist tradition. Unlike Nationalists, she saw Northern Ireland as separate and distinct from the Republic of Ireland. Besides, the stories her father told her about the Easter Rising and Ireland's fight for independence had no real meaning in Máiread's life—to her Ireland was a different country.

Máiread left school at the age of fourteen. She went to business school for a year, taking baby-sitting jobs to earn money. That year she also joined the Legion of Mary, a Catholic lay organization dedicated to helping the very poor in the Catholic community. (Catholic laypeople are those who work with the church, but are not members of the clergy, like priests or nuns.) As a member, Máiread worked primarily with children, especially handicapped children. She loved the work and devoted one or more evenings every week to it.

By the time she was sixteen, Máiread was working as an assistant bookkeeper in a textile factory in Belfast. When Máiread was eighteen years old, she and her family moved to a nearby neighborhood on the Falls Road called Andersonstown. It was yet another poor Catholic neighborhood. There Máiread was put in charge of one of the "cells," or groups, of the Legion of Mary. In the beginning only half a dozen adolescents belonged to her group, but under her leadership it eventually grew to as many as 150 teenagers.

The Northern Ireland of Máiread's childhood was quite different from Northern Ireland during "The Troubles" (the term the British coined to describe the conflict). While there were some isolated outbreaks of violence, these did not come close to the violence of the late 1960s and early 1970s. But everything changed for Máiread in 1968, when the civil rights movement in Northern Ireland began protesting the treatment of Catholics in Northern Ireland, and the Loyalists began to strike back. That year, the Corrigan family suffered their first blow as a result of the violence between Loyalists and Republicans. A car driven by a frightened motorist trying to flee one of the riots killed Máiread's niece, Michelle. The family was devastated.

When Loyalists began torching Catholic homes in Belfast, Máiread worked in church shelters helping those whose homes had been destroyed. As Máiread watched what was happening around her, her anger grew—and so did her fear. But she was determined not to be governed by her fear. While more and more young people became involved in the civil rights movement, Máiread's energy went into a different type of activism. She and other members of the Legion of Mary tried to serve their community. They arranged trips to the beach to get children and some teenagers away from the "hot spots" in order to keep them from getting involved in the violence. Despite their close proximity to the sea, many children had never seen it. People in the poorer sections of Belfast could not afford cars or even bus fare. Decaying, burned-out houses scarred their neighborhoods. There were few parks, playgrounds, or recreational facilities for children to play in. Vandals wrecked the few that existed.

During the early years of "The Troubles," Máiread tried to live as normal a life as possible. She enjoyed reading and studying religion. Evenings and Sundays were spent with the Legion of Mary members.

The burned out remains of a car are the aftermath of a riot in Derry, July 1996.

Saturdays she kept for herself, and she looked forward to spending the afternoons with her two nephews. During the summer, she would drive them to Lisburn, about ten miles from Belfast, where there was a swimming pool they could use.

Compared to many working-class Catholics in Northern Ireland, Máiread was lucky because she made a decent living. When she was twenty-one years old, she began working for the Guinness brewery, and she was quickly promoted to a good secretarial job. She had a car and lived comfortably. She also traveled frequently. Her volunteer work with the Legion of Mary took her to parts of the world most people, especially women from West Belfast, could never dream of visiting. In 1972, she traveled to Thailand to attend the World Council of Churches and she stayed in Bangkok for three weeks.

Máiread was the first woman to address the Chapter of Clergy in the conservative diocese of Belfast. The leadership and public speaking skills Máiread developed through her volunteer work would serve her well in her future work with the Peace People.

Like many Catholics in Belfast, Máiread suffered at the hands of the British army. Twice she spoke up when she saw British soldiers searching young girls. Each time she was beaten for her efforts. When she attended the funeral of a Republican, the service was interrupted when British soldiers threw tear gas through the church window. In another incident, Máiread's brother, Drew, was arrested while standing on a street corner one night. When the Corrigans anxiously phoned the army center to find out where Drew was, the army said they had never heard of him.

As a result of these experiences, Máiread came to understand why some young men would carry guns to protect themselves and their neighborhoods. She was so angry at the British army that she found herself wondering how she could get revenge. Should she join the Provos, the Provisional IRA? (The Provisional IRA resulted from a split in the IRA. The Provisional IRA is a paramilitary group; the official IRA moved away from violence.) In the face of such violence and mistreatment, it was something that nearly every Catholic in West Belfast wondered.

What are "human rights"?

Human rights are those rights that belong to all human beings. The right to life itself and the basic necessities of food and clothing are considered to be fundamental human rights. But the definition of human rights has broadened in the nineteenth and twentieth centuries. Human rights now make up three categories of rights for all people: individual rights, social rights, and collective rights.

Individual rights are the rights to life, liberty, privacy, the security of the individual, freedom of speech and press, freedom of worship, the right to own property, freedom from slavery, freedom from torture and unusual punishment, and similar rights, including those that are spelled out in the first ten amendments to the Constitution of the United States. Individual rights are based on the idea that the government should shield its citizens from any violations of these rights.

Social rights demand that governments provide such things as quality education, jobs, adequate medical care, housing, and other benefits. Basically, they call for a standard of living adequate for the health and well-being of the citizens of every nation.

Collective rights were spelled out in a document called the Universal Declaration of Human Rights, which was adopted by the General Assembly of the United Nations on December 10, 1948. This document proclaims the right of all human beings in the world to political, economic, social, and cultural self-determination; the right to peace; the right to live in a healthful and balanced environment; and the right to share in the earth's resources. The Universal Declaration of Human Rights also pledges the rights of life, liberty, and security of person—the basic individual human rights.

Instead of taking up arms, Máiread prayed for guidance. As she later recalled in the biography *Máiread Corrigan / Betty Williams*, she also spoke to a priest about what she could do to help stop the fighting. He told her that she should continue the work she was doing with the Legion of Mary. Máiread was frustrated with this answer. "But that's not enough!" she protested, "There's violence everywhere around us."

The priest suggested that she continue to pray for guidance. Máiread was in turmoil. As angry as she was at the British, she knew she did not believe in violence. As a Christian, she was challenged to follow the nonviolent example of Jesus Christ. She went to a church to pray and as she sat before the altar she recalled the words from the Bible, "Love your enemies. Do good to them that hurt you." She knew then that she could not harm another person, no matter what that person did to her. She became a committed pacifist.

With the Legion of Mary, Máiread began to visit prisoners in Long Kesh prison. Long Kesh, called "the Maze" by most Catholics, is a jail outside Belfast that contains a large number of Catholic and Protestant prisoners convicted of acts of terrorism. The Legion volunteers tried to remind the prisoners that they were Christians and that violence was not the way of Christ. Some of the prisoners criticized Máiread for her pacifism, saying that she chose the easy way out by doing nothing. But Máiread, having already struggled with her beliefs, remained steadfast in her conviction that violence was wrong.

In the summer of 1976 it seemed as if the violence that had gripped the country over the past seven

A British soldier in full combat gear walks past three young children on Belfast's Falls Road. Children in Northern Ireland have become accustomed to the presence of soldiers.

years would never end. The death toll that year reached a high of 300 people.

In Belfast, the capital of Northern Ireland, people had become accustomed to living in fear. No place was completely safe. Stores were bombed in the middle of the day, and children were killed on the way to school by stray bullets. In the evenings, extremists were known to knock on doors of homes and shoot whoever answered.

Máiread decided to escape the heat and violence and take a vacation on Achill Island, a popular vacation spot off the west coast of the Republic of Ireland. She cut her holiday short, however, to travel home with a friend who was grieving her mother's death from cancer. On August 10, she and her friend began the drive back to Belfast.

In the early afternoon of that same day, Anne

Corrigan Maguire was walking along Finaghy Road North with her four children. Joanne, aged eight-and-a-half, was on her bicycle; Mark, who would soon be seven, and John, aged two-and-a-half, were walking; and Andrew, six-weeks-old, was in a baby carriage. Just behind them walked Anne's sister, Eilish, and her two children. Suddenly, they heard gunshots. IRA snipers had shot at a British army patrol. They had missed, and two men, suspected of being the snipers, were speeding away in a car. Two army jeeps gave chase, and converged on the speeding car. The car, which was being driven by a young man named Danny Lennon, turned onto Finaghy Road North. The British soldiers opened fire, killing Danny instantly and seriously wounding his companion. The car careened toward the group walking on the sidewalk.

Eilish pushed her children out of the way. Mark also managed to get away. The car slammed into Anne and her other children, killing Joanne and Andrew instantly. John and Anne were critically injured.

As Máiread was driving home from Achill Island she heard on the radio about a tragedy in which two, perhaps three, children had been killed and their mother seriously injured when they were hit by a car after the driver had been killed by British soldiers. When she arrived home, she found out that the victims were her sister Anne and her niece and nephews. She raced to the hospital where Anne's husband, Jackie, and family members were waiting for news about Anne and John's condition. Anne was in a coma with a broken pelvis, two broken legs, and brain injuries. The doctors tried for hours to save young John, without success.

Jackie Maguire blamed the IRA completely for the accident. He believed that the British army was simply doing its job and he did not hesitate to denounce the IRA to the press. This was highly unusual. The IRA was not wholeheartedly supported by the Catholic population because some of their tactics—including burning an employment center, burning buses, and issuing bomb warnings—were injuring or disrupting the lives of other Catholics. But many people were too frightened to speak out against the IRA because they feared the IRA's retaliation. Jackie told reporters from the *Belfast Telegraph*, "If a lot of people were in a position to defend themselves against the Provisionals [the IRA] then maybe we would not be afraid." He continued, "I am afraid this incident will soon be forgotten by most people." He doubted that the deaths of his children would change anything in Northern Ireland.

As she listened to her brother-in-law, Máiread promised herself that she would do everything in her power to make sure this tragedy would not be forgotten—that something good would come out of it. Following Jackie's example, she also denounced the IRA to the press, telling a reporter from the *Belfast Telegraph*, "I am not afraid. They can do us no more harm. They have taken two of our children. These deaths won't have been in vain if they stop one kid from taking a gun and going out with it." Máiread went to a television station for an interview. She appealed to the people of Northern Ireland to put pressure on paramilitary groups to stop the violence. But as she spoke, she broke into tears and was unable to continue. Even the newscaster was so overcome with emotion that he had difficulty delivering the rest of the evening news. Máiread's interview was broadcast again twice that evening. Almost everyone in Northern Ireland saw or heard about it and few were left unmoved.

The only solace Máiread could find in this tragedy was the idea that somehow these deaths would bring about some change in Northern Ireland. Little did she know that in the same city, at the same moment, a young homemaker was also trying to set the wheels of change in motion.

Chapter 4

BETTY WILLIAMS: TAKING A STAND

Betty Williams was born the year before Máiread, in 1943, in Andersonstown, Belfast. Her father was a butcher and her mother a homemaker. She had one sister, Margaret, who was five years younger.

Betty's family heritage was rare for Northern Ireland. Her grandfathers, in particular, had unusual backgrounds. Her father's father was both a Protestant and a Republican. As a result, he suffered a great deal of employment discrimination in the Belfast shipyards even though he was highly skilled. Her mother's father was a Polish Jew who had lost most of his family during the Holocaust. In spite of his losses, he refused to feel bitterness and hatred over their deaths.

Betty's mother was a Catholic and her father was born a Protestant but converted to Catholicism when he was nineteen, about the same time he met Betty's mother. This rich heritage and nonsectarian spirit was passed down to Betty. Her family taught her to respect all people regardless of their nationality, race, or religion. Betty's family would not tolerate prejudice. Once her mother became angry with her for referring to someone as a Protestant. Her mother reprimanded her, saying, "I don't ever want to hear 'Catholic' or 'Protestant' in this house—Christian people is what we are."

Betty's parents were not wealthy, but this did not prevent Betty from having a happy childhood. She was very active and outgoing. When Betty was thirteen, her mother suffered a stroke that left her paralyzed. Betty became responsible for raising her sister, caring for her mother, and helping her father run the household. Because of her mother's paralysis, Betty and her father had to teach her mother how to walk and talk all over again.

Betty washed and fed her mother every morning before going to school and came home at lunch to cook and clean. After school she would do the shopping and more cooking. Her mother's stroke brought the family closer together and Betty's father became one of her closest friends. Her additional responsibilities gave her a maturity and strength that most children her age did not have. This strength would serve Betty well in her struggle for peace.

Betty was raised as a Catholic and attended Catholic school. Although she was not very interested in her school subjects, she loved to read. After school, she decided she was no longer interested in studying academics and, like Máiread, decided to attend a trade school where she took a two-year commercial course for secretaries.

Betty and Máiread's career choices were not unusual. Career opportunities in Northern Ireland in the 1960s were limited for women, particularly women from low-income backgrounds who could not afford college educations to prepare them for professional careers. Women from these backgrounds often held secretarial positions. Even college-educated women were often limited to nursing or teaching. Women's role in society was strongly bound by traditions that said women were expected to marry, have children, and stay at home to raise the family. The emerging feminist movement that had begun in the United States and England was suppressed in Northern Ireland. For women to fight for their own rights would have been seen as a betrayal to the Nationalist or Unionist cause. Women were expected to place these causes above their own struggle for equal rights.

Betty held a series of jobs as a teenager. Her jobs, in addition to her responsibilities at home, kept Betty very busy. She also began dating at a young age, and while still in her teens, she met a tall red-headed young man at a dance. His name was Ralph Williams and he worked as an engineer with the merchant marines, which meant he traveled on board large ships. His life must have seemed exciting and romantic to a girl who had so far lived her whole life in one neighborhood in Belfast. The two dated and quickly fell in love.

To complicate matters, Ralph was an Englishman and a Protestant. Betty and Ralph knew they could expect a hard time from both Catholics and Protestants. The Protestant and Catholic communities in Northern Ireland scorn interfaith marriages. Dating someone of a different religion can sometimes result in criticism and harassment. In fact, people have been killed for marrying someone of a different religion. But this did not deter Betty and Ralph. They were married on the island of Bermuda in 1961. Betty was eighteen years old.

Their son Paul was born two years later, and their daughter Deborah would be born in 1972. Betty settled into her role as homemaker. Ralph could be away from home for as many as eleven months out of the year, but after taking care of her mother, Betty

How are Protestants and Catholics in Northern Ireland different?

Lacking any physical characteristics to distinguish themselves, Protestants and Catholics have found other ways tell each other apart. Types of names are one way. Determining where someone lives is another good indicator because the communities are divided and tend to keep to themselves. Where a person goes to school or what sports teams they support can be a clue, since these are divided along sectarian lines as well. Schoolchildren who want to determine the religion of another child will ask him or her to recite a prayer called "The Lord's Prayer." While both Protestants and Catholics use this prayer, their versions differ slightly. In a country where religion is a primary means of identification this difference proves to be very important . Even the pronunciation of a letter carries weight. Catholics pronounce the letter "h" as "haytch" while Protestants pronounce it "aytch."

was used to taking responsibility. And she did get the benefit of travel because of his job. The family traveled to the United States and visited Miami and New York City. In 1964, Betty, Ralph, and Paul moved to Bermuda for a year when Ralph's job required him to be there.

When they returned from Bermuda, they moved into a two-family house in a middle-class neighborhood known as Finaghy. Betty loved their house and took great care in decorating it. Her hobbies included gardening, swimming, and reading every night. Two of her favorite authors were Leo Tolstoy and Charles Dickens.

Betty also worked outside of the home, taking secretarial or restaurant jobs. She felt these jobs were important because they gave her interests outside of the home and family. Betty had a very active intellect, and these jobs, like her reading, were one way she could keep learning. Like many other Catholics,

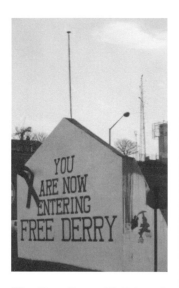

The Free Derry Wall is evidence of the division between the Unionists and Nationalists. The Unionists refer to the town as "Londonderry," while Nationalists call it "Derry" without the referral to the capital of England, London.

she experienced employment discrimination. She was turned down for a job after the would-be employers found out that, despite her Protestant-sounding name, she was really a Catholic.

When the Provisional IRA was founded, Betty found herself sympathizing with the group. She had seen the ways the Royal Ulster Constabulary and the British army had abused Catholics. The British army ransacked her sister's home during one of their searches. Betty was deeply affected by the injustices she saw around her, and she shared the deep frustration and anger that Catholics were feeling. She felt that the IRA was the only group that would protect the Catholic community.

Betty herself experienced the British army's mistreatment of Catholics. She was driving home late one night from her waitressing job when she was stopped by the British army. They arrested her and brought her to a military barrack where she was interrogated. Her arrest was based on a case of mistaken identity. The British thought she was someone else who was linked to the recent murder of a Protestant on the Falls Road.

The violence in Northern Ireland took the lives of two of Betty's cousins. Her eighteen-year-old cousin, Danny, was shot on his doorstep by Protestant extremists. Another cousin was killed by a booby-trapped car parked by the side of the road. The IRA had left it there and it exploded just as Betty's cousin drove past. Betty, the daughter of two people whose love crossed the Protestant-Catholic divide, had loved ones killed by each side of that divide.

The British government's decision in 1972 to govern Northern Ireland directly did not help to end the violence. Belfast was still a war zone and people lived in fear. The bombings continued. Throughout Belfast there were the charred remains of buildings that had been destroyed by fire or bombs.

It seemed that no place was safe. People were not even safe in their own homes. Paramilitaries were known to knock on people's doors late at night and storm into the house, killing the people inside. People could not go about their day-to-day lives without some reminder of the violence. Armored vehicles patrolled the streets. Soldiers with rifles stood on street corners. In the main shopping area of Belfast the RUC patted down people and checked their bags for weapons or explosives. It was not unusual for drivers to be stopped by a roadblock and be questioned about where they were going while their car was checked for explosives. Many roads were blocked by huge stone squares called "dragon's teeth," which

A roadblock checkpoint where police search motorists and their cars for weapons and explosives.

prevented fast getaways. Even walking to school or playing on the street was not safe. Children had been killed by stray bullets.

People traveling through Northern Ireland could tell whether they were in friendly or hostile territory by looking at the roadside curbs or telephone poles. If these were painted red, white, and blue, the colors of the British flag, it was Loyalist territory. If they were painted green, white, and orange, the color of the Irish flag, it was a Republican neighborhood.

People learned that there were certain things they should not do: do not open your door if someone knocks late at night, do not go into certain sections of town, do not go near a car that appears abandoned—it could be a car bomb. Do not leave your own car unattended or the British army might suspect it is a car bomb and destroy it.

Like most people in Northern Ireland, Betty became accustomed to living with danger. Eventually she realized that all of the violence was only causing more violence and innocent lives were being lost. She had always opposed the British army and the RUC. Now she also began to question the IRA. Their motto was, "Peace with justice." She could not see the justice in their actions. What she did see was young teenagers taking up violence for the IRA's cause and innocent people being killed by bombs and bullets.

A turning point for Betty occurred when she saw a British soldier killed. She was looking into a store window when she heard gunfire. She turned to look, and saw the soldier fall nearby. She was struck by how young he was—no more than twenty years old. She knelt down next to the dying boy and whispered a prayer in his ear. After the army took away his body, some Catholic women angrily confronted her for showing compassion to the "enemy." Suddenly Betty realized how insignificant human life had become in this conflict.

Betty joined a short-lived peace group called Witness for Peace. Reverend Joseph Parker, a Protestant clergyman, whose thirteen-year-old son was killed by IRA bombs, founded the group. Reverend Parker emigrated to North America a few years later, frustrated in his efforts to bring an end to the violence. But he made a huge impact on Betty, giving her a first taste of the effort to end violence through peaceful means.

A British army soldier stands in front of Irish Republican Army (IRA) graffiti spray-painted on a building.

Betty wanted to do something about the violence, but did not know exactly how to go about it. Among her friends and neighbors she spoke out against both the injustices and the violence she saw around her. She tried to persuade some IRA members she knew to give up violence, and in some cases she was successful—but it was not enough. She knew she could do more.

On August 10, 1976, Betty was driving with her four-year-old daughter, Deborah, on Finaghy Road North and came upon the scene of Anne Maguire's accident as emergency crews and the army were gathering up the victims to take to the hospital. The scene—a broken and mangled bike, a baby carriage, and the bodies of children and their mother—was devastating.

When Betty arrived home, she was so upset she could not concentrate on anything else. She turned on the news even though she knew she would only see a televised image of the carnage she had just witnessed herself on Finaghy Road. She called the doctor to find out what to do for her daughter, who was dazed after what she had just seen, and then she put Deborah to bed.

For years Betty had lived in fear of the violence and had done little to try to change the situation, but that evening something inside her snapped. Suddenly she grabbed a writing pad and drove to Andersonstown. She began knocking on doors, asking people "Do you want peace?" When they replied yes, she asked them to sign a petition condemning the IRA's violence and demanding that the IRA leave their neighborhoods. Within a matter of minutes she had collected 100 signatures. As she went from door to door, women came out of their homes to help her gather signatures. By now the news of the Maguire children's deaths had been broadcast all over Northern Ireland, and everyone was horrified by the tragedy. Mothers knew that something like this could easily have happened to their own families, and when Betty knocked on their doors challenging them to do something about the violence, they were ready to work for change. Like the Pied Piper, Betty walked through the streets of Andersonstown followed by a growing crowd of women who had left their homes to follow her through the streets. Soon there were 100 women helping Betty with her petition. As they collected signatures and exchanged phone numbers they resolved to join together and stop the violence.

When they ran out of paper, they kept collecting signatures on whatever scraps they could find. When Betty returned home, the women went with her. They counted signatures through the night and into the morning. They had 6,000 signatures.

Betty called the local newspaper and informed them of the petition demanding that the IRA stop its campaign of violence. When she told the reporter who answered the phone how many signatures she had collected, he did not believe her. She invited him to come down to her house the see the signatures piled on chairs, tables, and floors. Within hours, Betty's house was overrun with journalists. Speaking of the petition she told the *Belfast Telegraph*, "This is a cry from the heart . . . because we believe that what happened to the Maguire family on Monday could have happened to any one of us women out walking our children. Believe me, I am afraid myself—I am terrified, but this has got to stop."

In an interview later with the *Irish Times*, Betty recalled being exhausted from lack of sleep and talking to reporters. One of the journalists who came to interview Betty made a strong impression on her. He came over and asked her if she would like a cup of tea. She gratefully said yes. When he handed her the tea he said, "I've been waiting for someone like you to happen for seven years." His name was Ciaran McKeown and he was a journalist for the *Irish News*. Little did either one of them know how important they would become to each over the next few years.

As news of the petition spread, women began collecting signatures on their own and exchanging phone numbers. They all agreed they wanted to do something about the violence that took the lives of the Maguire children.

On Thursday evening, Betty Williams appeared on television, where she read the petition demanding that the IRA stop its military campaign. She announced that there would be a mass rally on Saturday afternoon on Finaghy Road, where the Maguire children had been killed. She invited all women, Protestant and Catholic, to join this new movement to protest *all* paramilitary violence, and she gave out her phone number.

Máiread heard about Betty's petition and called to thank her and to invite her to join the Corrigan and Maguire families at the children's funeral the next day. Just before the funeral ceremony at the Church of St. Michael, Betty and Máiread were introduced. The two women liked each other instantly.

Family, friends, and hundreds of strangers followed the hearse containing the three tiny, white coffins, covered in roses, in a procession from the church to the cemetery. Of the Corrigan-Maguire family, only Anne was absent. She was still in the hospital in a coma. Thousands of people, both Protestant and Catholic, lined the streets, united in grief over these senseless deaths. The news media were also there, ready to relay events to a world stunned by the tragedy.

After the funeral, Máiread arranged to meet Betty at the rally the next day. She still had one thing left to do. Gathering some of the roses from the children's coffins, she walked alone to the home of Danny Lennon, the driver of the car that had killed the Maguire children. She did not know what she was going to say. She half expected to have the door slammed in her face, but instead she was greeted by the tear-stained face of Danny's mother. Mrs. Lennon had just been writing a letter to Anne Maguire trying to apologize for what her son had done. Máiread gave Mrs. Lennon the roses and told her she mourned the death of Danny and shared the grief of his family.

The following day almost 10,000 people descended upon Andersonstown for the Finaghy Road North demonstration. People came on foot and by car. Some Protestant women even chartered a bus. When Betty found out that people from the Protestant area of

Belfast were crossing the sectarian divide to participate in the rally, she cried. While the demonstrators were mostly women, there were some men and children in attendance as well. The women carried placards with the names of their neighborhoods, including the Protestant areas of Shankill and East Belfast. Some IRA supporters stood off to the side watching. When the Protestant participants arrived, they began to harass them, calling them names. The name-calling turned to jostling and pushing. As the marchers headed toward the cemetery, the IRA supporters locked arms to form a wall through which the marchers would have to pass. Some women who tried to pass through were punched. IRA supporters began to chant, "Brits Out! Provos Rule!" But when the Protestant women emerged from the crowd of angry IRA supporters, they were welcomed and embraced by their fellow marchers. Other angry marchers, most of them Catholic, drove off the IRA crowd. The media were there to record all of it.

Attending the demonstration took tremendous courage for both the Protestants and Catholics. For a Protestant to travel to Catholic neighborhood was to risk her or his life. For a Catholic to stand up to the IRA was to be labeled a traitor.

The large crowd assembled at the scene of the accident, where they sang hymns and prayed. Then they had a moment of silence for the dead Maguire children. When the demonstration broke up, Catholics escorted the Protestants back to their buses to make sure there was no more trouble from the supporters of the IRA.

The rally had been a huge success, greater than Máiread or Betty could have imagined. For the first

Headstone of IRA volunteer Danny Lennon who is buried in Milltown Cemetary, Belfast. His death on August 10, 1976, was one of many that inspired the peace movement founded by Betty Williams and Máiread Corrigan.

time, the women of Belfast had raised their voices as one to cry, "Stop!" and Máiread and Betty vowed that this cry would not die away as emotions cooled. They wanted more than a peace demonstration. They wanted a peace movement.

That night a group of Republican extremists tried to burn down Betty's house. They were chased away by her neighbors. The next morning the sun rose to reveal walls in Andersonstown painted with the slogans, "Betty Is a Traitor" and "Kill Those Who Are Not With Us." But Betty and Máiread refused to let these threats stop them. They refused to live in fear.

The Finaghy Road demonstration on August 14, 1976, attracted 10,000 supporters from both Protestant and Catholic areas of Belfast.

Chapter 5

THE GUERRILLAS OF PEACE

In a matter of a few short days, two women from the working-class district of Belfast had released a flood of yearning for peace that would have been unthinkable only one week before. The question that now faced Betty and Máiread was what to do with the momentum they had started at the Finaghy Road rally. They met to discuss the march and the possibility of more peace demonstrations. The journalist Ciaran McKeown offered his help. Ciaran was a Catholic from Derry who had been very active in the civil rights movement.

At first, Máiread had mixed emotions about their plans. She was shaken by the loss of her nephews and niece and terribly worried about her sister Anne. Still she could not shake the memory of the previous day, when thousands came together to pray for peace. She knew these people would need someone to lead them, motivating them to take to the streets and demonstrate for an end to the violence.

Ciaran made out a plan for the movement that consisted of two phases. The first phase would be a series of marches to be held throughout Northern Ireland and in key cities in Britain and Ireland. Betty, Máiread, and Ciaran would encourage others to organize peace demonstrations in their own towns and neighborhoods. The next phase would consist of coordinating and supporting these local peace communities. Unlike politicians, who tried to win peace at the top so that it would reach down to ordinary citizens, this plan would work for peace from the ground up. It would be what is called a "grassroots" movement. Peace would flow from the citizens to the policy makers.

When Ciaran presented his plan for the first phase to Betty and Máiread, they thought it was much too ambitious. Ciaran had a rally planned almost every week. But he pointed out that the program of rallies would give people an immediate sense of the sweeping nature and importance of this peace movement. Betty and Máiread were up for the challenge. They also agreed that they wanted to invite men to participate in the movement, which so far had brought out mostly women.

The three held a press conference at the Church of St. Michael's to announce their new peace initiative. Minutes before addressing the media, they agreed upon a statement of purpose. Ciaran suggested they call it their "declaration," to be read at every rally. They all agreed to the name "Peace People," and the hastily written statement became "The Declaration of the Peace People."

Meanwhile the IRA stepped up its campaign of fear. During the week leading up to the next march, IRA supporters circulated fliers throughout Andersonstown warning residents that if they turned against the IRA it could cost them their lives. It was obvious that the paramilitaries were already beginning to feel pressure from this new peace initiative.

Their first rally as the Peace People was held in Ormeau Park, near a Protestant area of Belfast. Women from the Protestant area made thousands of leaflets and slipped them through the mail slots of

What is the Declaration of the Peace People?

We have a simple message for the world from this movement for peace. We want to live and love and build a just and peaceful society. We want for our children, as we want for ourselves, our lives at home, at work and at play, to be lives of joy and peace. We recognize that there are many problems in society which are a source of conflict and violence. We recognize that every bullet fired and every exploding bomb makes that work more difficult. We reject the use of the bomb and bullet and all the techniques of violence. We dedicate ourselves to working with our neighbors, near and far, day in and day out, to building that peaceful society in which the tragedies we have known are a bad memory and a continuing warning.

houses to spread the word about the rally. On August 24, thousands of people joined Betty and Máiread and marched up the Ormeau Road. As they poured into the park they could see thousands more already gathered on the soccer fields at the north end of the park.

As the park filled, someone began singing a hymn. The song was taken up by those close by and traveled back to the groups at the edge of the park. Protestant women greeted and hugged Catholic women. Máiread made a short speech encouraging the citizens of the Republic of Ireland to join the marches. There was no loudspeaker equipment so she had to use a megaphone to address the huge crowd. At the end of the rally Máiread announced that the Peace People had been invited by the Protestant women of the Shankill area to march from the Falls Road to the Shankill Road and into the nearby Woodvale Park.

The crowd fell silent. Catholics had never been invited into a Protestant area before and for Protestants to invite them now was a tremendous gesture of goodwill toward the peace movement. As the

The Shankill Road, Belfast, with a Loyalist mural supporting the Ulster Volunteer Force, a Protestant paramilitary group. The Shankill Road is a primarily Protestant section of Belfast.

crowd absorbed the magnitude of what Máiread had said, they erupted into cheers. The Peace People were off to a great start. The next day pictures from the march appeared in newspapers throughout the world. In breaching the sectarian divide, the Peace People were making history, a fact not lost on people all over the globe.

The following Saturday was beautiful and sunny as the Peace People prepared to embark on one of the most symbolically significant of their marches. They were to cross a divide that had been considered impassable. Because the two sides seemed irreconcilable, the British army had actually erected walls to keep the Protestant and Catholic communities apart. Called "peace lines," they were walls made of corrugated iron, barbed wire, or red brick. Many peace lines have military checkpoints where the British army stop cars to check for weapons and explosives.

Peace Lines were constructed to prevent violent outbreaks between the divided communities. This peace line is located on the Shankill Road.

Many residents of the Catholic Falls Road area supported the marchers. But as the marchers left the Falls Road and entered the Shankill Road, IRA supporters began throwing rocks and shouting "Traitors!" at the marchers. Once again the sheer number of peace demonstrators overwhelmed them and they were forced to stop.

On the Shankill Road Protestant residents turned out to cheer on the marchers. One man ran up, kissed a nun, and shouted, "Youse are doin' a fine job." In Woodvale Park, the demonstrators gathered in front of a small hill on which loudspeaker equipment had been mounted. Sadie Patterson, a Protestant and president of Women Together—another organization working for reconciliation—stepped up to the microphone. She welcomed the demonstrators and sang a hymn. Máiread spoke next followed by Betty. Church bells rang out in celebration while people wept tears of joy.

As a leader of the Peace People, Betty was discovering skills she never knew she had. While Máiread already had experience in public speaking and leadership through her work with the Legion of Mary, Betty did not. She had always been motivated and outspoken and these proved to be great leadership skills. She also discovered that she had a gift for speaking in public. Described as an "explosive" and "impulsive" woman, her warmth, enthusiasm, and dedication to peace were contagious.

After the success of these first rallies, Máiread, Betty, and Ciaran realized they would need office space. Up to this point the Peace People had been operating out of Betty's home. With volunteers coming and going and the phone ringing constantly, it was putting a strain on her family. Ciaran went to see Reverend Ray Davey of the Corrymeela Reconciliation Center in Belfast. Reverend Davey offered the Peace People office space for their movement for as long as they needed.

The Peace People announced their complete plan for upcoming rallies and the office was deluged with calls asking for information. Many people who called offered to help organize. Peace groups were springing up throughout the country.

The next rally was to be held in Londonderry, as it is known by Unionists, or Derry, as it is called by Nationalists. The second-largest city in Northern Ireland, it is located about seventy-five miles northeast of Belfast. At first glance Derry appears quite unlike industrial Belfast. Hugging both sides of the River Foyle and gently climbing the surrounding hills, Derry looks like a pretty European city. A second glance reveals the similarities between these two cities. Like Belfast, Derry is scarred by bomb blasts and arson and is completely divided between Protestants and Catholics.

The city is a painful example of Catholic oppression. Catholics are the majority in Derry, but during the 1970s they were still governed by a Protestant minority. Derry also has one of the poorest Catholic communities in Northern Ireland, called the Bogside. The Protestant community lives across the river in a community called Waterside. The communities are so separated that many people believe the division can never by repaired.

It was in this city that the "Troubles" began when the RUC attacked peaceful civil rights protesters and rioting began. It was also in Derry that the "Troubles" reached one of its lowest points on Bloody Sunday.

Ciaran had carefully selected the location of the march, the Craigavon Bridge, which connects the Bogside with the Waterside. In a moving gesture of reconciliation, the marchers approached from each side of the river and met in the middle of the bridge. Over 20,000 people showed up for the march from all over Northern Ireland and as far away as Dublin. Off to the side, the police and the army stood watching, ready to intervene in case of any disorder. Under the bridge patrol boats passed constantly to make sure that no one would try to bomb the bridge. Even this joyful gathering of thousands of peaceful demonstrators was not without the threat of danger.

In spite of the genuine desire for reconciliation that had been displayed during the rally, the residents of Derry still returned to opposite sides of the river knowing that as much as they demonstrated and worked for peace, some of their neighbors still believed in violence. But for a few minutes on the bridge, both Protestants and Catholics were able to forget the bombings, the sectarian murders, the discrimination, grief, and hatred, and grasp at a hope that had eluded them for years—the hope for peace.

As the movement gathered steam, Máiread and Betty became the targets of increased criticism. People began to wonder who was paying for the chartered buses and printed pamphlets. Was there some

The Craigavon Bridge, Derry, spans the River Foyle and connects the Bogside with the Waterside.

other organization behind the Peace People? These suspicions were encouraged by the paramilitary organizations. They tried to find ways to denounce the peace movement. The Protestant extremists attacked them for not taking sides against the IRA. The IRA, on the other hand, felt the Peace People were pro-British because they did not denounce the British army or the Protestant paramilitary organizations. They said that the Peace People demanded "peace at any price" not "peace with justice." The IRA asserted that they wanted peace as well, but only after Catholics had achieved justice. They believed that if they stopped their violent attacks, the oppression and discrimination would never end. The Unionists opposed the Peace People because rumors began to circulate that the British government or the British army was financing the movement so that once peace was achieved Britain could withdraw from Northern Ireland. Even some politicians felt threatened by the strength of the movement, because it reminded them of their own failure to win peace.

Betty, Máiread, and Ciaran tried to dispel these rumors, insisting that they were not against the IRA, but instead against all forms of violence. As Betty and Máiread told the *Belfast Telegraph*, "We say now, for all time, that our peace drive is against all violence." Regarding their ties to the government, the leaders of the Peace People refused to align themselves with any political party. When a reporter from the *Manchester Guardian*, a British newspaper, wrote "ordinary people do not stop wars, politicians do," Betty responded, "Yes, the politicians will end it, but what we're doing is showing that the ordinary people of Ulster do want it to stop."

Many Catholics still supported the IRA, believing that it was the only organization that could protect them. They had not forgotten how Catholics had suffered at the hands of the RUC and the British army. They grew angry with the Peace People.

This feeling reached a climax on October 10 after the death of a young boy who had been hit by a plastic bullet shot by a British soldier. A meeting was called in a community center in one of Belfast's Catholic neighborhoods to protest the boy's death. Máiread and Betty, and Betty's husband, Ralph, were invited to the meeting. When they stepped onto the platform, some people began to shout "Out, Out!" at them. When Máiread went forward to speak she was drowned out by shouting. Ralph and Betty tried to leave but were attacked by an angry mob. Máiread stayed on the platform, hoping she would still have a chance to speak. She had planned to denounce the army's violence. However, order was never restored and she eventually gave up and left the platform, only to be attacked as well.

In spite of the injuries they suffered, both Máiread and Betty were glad that they had attended the meeting. They wanted to show that they were opposed to all violence, both British and Irish. They each publicly forgave their attackers. Betty told the *London Times,* "It was a totally emotional reaction and I do not hold any malice against the people who attacked us. . . . If I had lost a thirteen-year-old boy like that I would have been upset as well."

In addition to the death threats and attacks, Betty and Máiread suffered under the strain of constantly being in the spotlight of the media. The pressure was enormous. Anything they said could be broadcast on television or appear in the following day's newspaper. Reporters continually hounded them for interviews, leaving them no time for themselves or their families.

Betty and Máiread also traveled constantly, trying to educate the world abroad about the nature of the conflict in Northern Ireland and their organization. Their lives as well as Ciaran's had changed completely in a matter of weeks and they had no time to adjust to their international fame. But the three of them remained firm in their commitment to work for peace.

Máiread, Betty, and Ciaran continually drew strength and inspiration from the people who supported their cause. Their decision to speak out and demand peace was contagious and thousands took up the call. Peace groups were forming throughout Northern Ireland, even in the most dangerous areas of Belfast. In mid-September, there was a spontaneous demonstration of Protestant women in Belfast against the activity of one of the Protestant paramilitary groups, the Ulster Defense Association (UDA). The UDA had hijacked and set fire to two buses. Thirty angry women blocked a road to protest, stopping traffic. And in Belfast, the use of the confidential telephone had increased since the Peace People began. The confidential telephone is a telephone that people can use in secrecy to inform the police of paramilitary activity.

The Peace People had the reassurance that their message of peace was being heard throughout the world. Communities of Peace People were starting up in Europe and America. People from various peace organizations throughout the world would descend upon Northern Ireland to attend the Peace People rallies and show their support.

The Falls Park, Belfast, march on October 23 was

Fire bombs are frequently used during rioting. On some streets the burned-out body of a car is not an uncommon sight.

one of the most memorable—and also one of the most difficult—of the Peace People's rallies. The Protestants crossed the peace line into the Catholic Falls Road area. Both Protestants and Catholics feared what might be in store for them along their route through this volatile section of Belfast. But the marchers refused to let fear stop them from doing what they knew was right.

The Peace People declared this march the greatest victory for peace. Both Protestants and Catholics overcame their fear to penetrate the heart of IRA territory and demand peace. Under attack, the Peace People drew closer together and demonstrated their commitment to nonviolence. The marchers gained new self-respect as they proved they would not be intimidated. The attack only motivated them to work for peace with renewed vigor. In the Peace People's magazine, *Peace by Peace*, one member referred to the Falls Road rally as, "the march everyone remembers. 'I was on the Falls Road that day' they say and it appears to be almost a badge of merit to say that."

The marches continued through October and November and so did Betty and Máiread's hectic pace. They were exhausted but found the work extremely satisfying. Along with the marches in Northern Ireland, the Peace People were holding marches throughout Britain, which proved to be just as successful. The final rally in Great Britain was to be held in London on November 27. The march was to be from Hyde Park to Trafalgar Square in the heart of London.

Because this march was to be held in such a large city, with thousands of tourists adding to the city's population, careful preparations needed to be made. Ciaran, Betty, and Máiread decided they had better spend the week leading up to the march in London. The week was completely monopolized by the press. By now, Máiread and Betty had enough experience to handle the press with a great deal of skill. They never prepared speeches or comments in advance. Instead they spoke spontaneously, directly, and from the heart. The two women complemented each other well. Betty came across as the no-nonsense, tough personality while Máiread was gentler and more charming. Audiences loved them.

On the day of the march, thousands of marchers from the United Kingdom and as far away as Scandinavia, Holland, Germany, France, the United States, and Canada assembled on the grass at London's huge Hyde Park. As always, there were a few supporters of the IRA present, shouting "Peace with justice," but they were soon drowned out in the noise of the crowd.

Betty, Máiread, and Ciaran, led the march. Also in attendance was Joan Baez, the famous folksinger and civil rights activist.

The marchers left the park and passed behind Buckingham Palace, home to the English monarchs. They were preceded by a light blue police van while above them flew a police helicopter. They stopped before Westminster Abbey, England's most famous church, and the leaders went into the cathedral to pay their respects to the Archbishop of Canterbury and the Archbishop of Westminster, both leaders of the Protestant Church in England, and Cardinal Hume, head of the Catholic Church in England. The clergymen spontaneously joined the march.

At Trafalgar Square a large crowd was waiting for them. The leaders and those who had been invited moved up to the platform.

Massed to the right of the platform were two groups opposed to the march: pacifists who demanded the withdrawal of British troops in Northern Ireland and supporters of the IRA. When Betty, Máiread, and Ciaran arrived, the opposition groups began shouting and continued to do so throughout the rally. When their shouting made it hard to hear the speakers, the police began to move them away from the area. There were a few confrontations and four people were arrested.

The rally began with a hymn, then the Archbishop of Canterbury led everyone in reciting the Lord's Prayer. The Archbishop of Westminster read a passage from the Bible. Afterwards, everyone joined in singing a song written by a man from Derry and dedicated to the Peace People entitled "Peace." Still the opposition continued shouting.

The speeches began. The first to speak was Diana Rigg, a famous British actress, and she read peace poems written by children in Belfast. When Máiread stepped up to the platform, she was tense and began somewhat hesitantly. But as she spoke from her heart her voice gathered strength as she declared, "We have had war for seven years, and we have made mistakes. Not one of the victims deserved to die. We must never repeat our errors. We offer a hope, a vision. We will unite our people, and we will establish peace in Ulster. Help us!" The crowd burst into wild applause.

When Ciaran spoke he also asked for help in bringing about an end to the violence in Northern Ireland. In a speech that drew inspiration from Martin Luther King, Jr., and was quoted in the *Irish Times*, he stated, "This movement is not just a cry of anguish. We are asserting that there be another way forward. The war may continue. We will have to work on for peace." He concluded, "This time, we shall overcome."

Each time someone spoke, the hecklers shouted out obscenities. When Joan Baez got up and sang some folksongs about peace, she was nearly drowned out, but the crowd joined in singing and drowned out the hecklers.

Finally it was Betty's turn to speak. All throughout the rally she had been glaring at the hecklers. Betty walked up to the microphone and when the hecklers began shouting she turned on them. "Shout louder," she yelled. "We can't hear you! Louder! You'll lose your voices and then we won't hear you at all!"

At the Trafalgar Square march on November 27, 1976, in London, police grappled with a heckler opposed to the views of the Peace People.

The crowd laughed and applauded. During her speech, thanking those who had come to the march, she continued to taunt the hecklers. "Well, well! We can't hear them anymore! Ladies and gentlemen, we are now going to take up a collection to buy them some throat lozenges!" Betty and the Peace People had refused to be intimidated by bricks and stones. They certainly were not going to be frightened by a group of hecklers.

When Betty finished the crowd gave her a triple "Hip, hip, hurrah!" and with that the march was over. The size of the crowd was estimated to be about 15,000 people. The Peace People rallies in Great Britain were brought to a close.

Even after the unusually hectic week in London, Ciaran, Betty, and Máiread still could not take time to rest. The next day they had to fly to Norway to pick up the first large donation to their cause. The Norwegian press and several civic organizations were so impressed by Máiread and Betty's work that they took up a national collection to raise money for the Peace People. They collected over $340,000, and the money was to be presented to the three leaders as a special Norwegian People's Peace Prize.

The prize money was desperately needed to help support several of the Peace People's programs. Already they supplied meals for the aged, social activities for youth, and help for working mothers. Betty, Máiread, and Ciaran believed that peace would be achieved through increased community networks: people talking to each other across the Protestant/Catholic divide and learning how to live together. These contributions helped to establish these networks.

Betty and Máiread rode together in a taxi. Betty was very upset. Only two hours before, Ralph had been rushed to a hospital with an acute attack of appendicitis. When they arrived at the airport, Betty refused to board the plane for Norway. She wanted to stay with her husband. Máiread and Ciaran finally persuaded her that Ralph was being well taken care of in the hospital and there was nothing she could do for him. They caught the plane just in time. Once again, Betty's duty to the Peace People took her away from her family.

After the presentation of Norwegian People's Peace Prize December 10, 1976, in Oslo, Norway, the founders of the Peace People, Betty Williams (left kneeling), Máiread Corrigan (center), and Ciaran McKeown (right), are congratulated by local children.

Chapter 6
THE PEACE PEOPLE MAKE PROGRESS

It is hard to imagine a landmark that holds more symbolism in the Northern Irish conflict than the River Boyne. It was here, in 1690, that the troops of King William of Orange, a Protestant, defeated those of King James, a Catholic. The Protestant Orange Order in Northern Ireland celebrates the anniversary of the battle every July. The first few weeks of July are called "marching season," as the Orange Order, a Unionist organization, parades throughout Northern Ireland, even in Catholic areas. These marches renew paramilitary violence every year.

Ironically, the Boyne is located in the Republic of Ireland, about twenty-five miles north of Dublin, and is a place most Orangemen—Protestant Unionists— would never go. In fact, many Northern Irish Protestants have never visited the Republic.

Upon their return from Norway, Betty, Máiread, and Ciaran immediately had to prepare for the Peace People rally on the banks of the River Boyne. They had brought together Protestant and Catholic, by crossing the peace line. They had joined Irish and English by holding rallies in England. Now they would bring together Ireland and Northern Ireland by gathering on the banks of the Boyne.

Sunday, December 5, was a cold, damp day. A thick fog blanketed the area as the buses and cars left Belfast for the two-hour trip to Drogheda, a city on the banks of the river. Betty, Ciaran, Joan Baez, and

Orangemen marching in a tribute to William of Orange, the Protestant king who defeated the Catholics in Ireland.

a few other invited guests rode in the same car from Belfast. Máiread followed in another car, talking to reporters.

The buses stopped at the edge of Drogheda. A new bridge had been opened a few months earlier in the center of the city. It had been named the Bridge of Peace. The rally was to take place on the southern side of the bridge. The marchers from Northern Ireland would cross the bridge to join marchers from the Republic of Ireland. Everyone huddled together trying to keep warm as they waited for the march to begin.

The marchers made their way through the city. In the distance, the blurred outline of the bridge could barely be seen through the dense fog. As they drew closer to the bridge, the sun became visible and when they reached the bridge the fog lifted, leaving the marchers drenched in sunlight.

The Northern Irish marchers filled all four entrances on the north side of the bridge as they approached the marchers from the Republic of Ireland. They came to a halt about 100 yards from each other. The leaders made their way forward, then the two crowds raced to greet each other. People shook hands, hugged, kissed, and threw themselves into the arms of total strangers. They cried, talked, and exchanged phone numbers and addresses. The banners from Shankill and East Belfast in Northern Ireland—Protestant neighborhoods— flew next to banners from the counties of Cork and Galway in the predominantly Catholic Republic of Ireland.

The ceremony began. Once again hymns were sung, prayers and speeches were said, and the Declaration of the Peace People was read. The speeches from the three leaders followed. Máiread's speech summed up the message of the Peace People: "Let's say on the sixth December the Irish people began a new battle. A battle to replace war with peace, hatred with love, anger with friendship, injustice with justice, people without homes with homes, unemployment with jobs. Let us dedicate ourselves to this new form of battle that can turn Ireland back into a land of saints and scholars." She sat down to the cheers of the crowd.

Ciaran spoke next. He told the crowd that what the Peace People had accomplished so far was not enough. Ciaran declared, "We are seeking something far, far more than mere peace. We want a nonviolent society that will show the world that peace is possible."

During Betty's speech she thanked all who had attended the march. In particular, she pointed out a group of Protestant women from Northern Ireland who had never been to the Republic before. She introduced supporters who had come from as far away as Canada, the United States, Sweden, Germany, and Norway. The *Irish Times* estimated the attendance at this march to be between 12,000 and 15,000.

The Peace People closed 1976 with the rest of the scheduled marches, holding their final rally in Belfast only two days before Christmas. In only four and half months this organization had scheduled a successful series of rallies that were attended by over 100,000 people. It had put together a peace organization with thousands of members, not only in Northern Ireland, but throughout Europe, the United States, and Canada. The group had also launched a magazine entitled *Peace by Peace*, which was selling well at newsstands. But as Ciaran said, it was not enough. The hard work of building peace still lay ahead. The Peace People now had to concentrate on the second phase of the movement: coordinating and supporting the activities of the 106 peace groups that had been formed in Northern Ireland alone. Each group would carry out specific projects in its area that would try to bring Protestants and Catholics together.

Betty and Máiread also continued to travel abroad, especially to Canada and the United States, in an attempt to stop the flow of money to Northern Ireland's paramilitary groups. They had begun this effort on a trip to the United States the previous October. Some members of the Irish communities in the United States and Canada provide a great deal of money to support the armed struggle in Northern Ireland.

While in the states they gave almost continuous

How do Irish Americans feel about the conflict in Northern Ireland?

After the Potato Famine, emigration from Ireland continued as economic pressures such as unemployment forced people to find jobs in other countries. Emigration and the breakup of the family became a sad fact of life, especially in the farming communities in the west of Ireland. Most emigrants traveled to England, the United States, Canada, and Australia, knowing they would never see Ireland or their families again.

The Irish who came to the United States in the nineteenth century were not accepted by society and were discriminated against. Feeling unwelcome in this new country only increased the Irish people's longing for their homeland, and they maintained an active interest in Ireland's welfare.

Over the years the Irish in the United States began to succeed and grow prosperous, but they never forgot their ties to their ancestral homeland. In fact, many have used their success and prosperity to try to help Ireland and the conflict in Northern Ireland. Several organizations have been founded by Irish Americans to support improvement projects in Ireland, and to work for peace in Northern Ireland. Irish-American influence has also brought subsidiaries of U.S. companies to Ireland and Northern Ireland, providing necessary jobs. As a result, Irish Americans have become a powerful, vocal force in the affairs of Northern Ireland and Ireland. In fact they played a vital role in the peace talks that ultimately led to the 1998 Northern Ireland Peace Agreement.

However, there are many Irish Americans who, removed from the conflict in Northern Ireland, do not understand the true causes of the violence. They believe that the hostility is based on religious differences rather than political and economic hardships.

Irish Republicanism is alive and well in the Irish-American community and it is no secret that a great deal of the IRA's money to buy weapons and explosives comes from American wallets.

An Irish boy holds an American and Irish flag to greet the President of the United States, Bill Clinton. Many Irish emigrated to the United States during the Potato Famine, but their families have continued to share a bond with Ireland.

interviews to television and newspapers. When reporters asked Máiread and Betty if they feared for their lives, they replied that they were not afraid. With cold realism, Betty told the *London Times*, "Before this finishes, we will see the most atrocious acts of violence in Northern Ireland . . . I fully expect that." But she added, "One has to forget about oneself. Peace is going to be much harder to achieve than war was to start in Northern Ireland."

The first few months of 1977 were spent putting together a formal constitution for the organization and attending to finances. The group had been receiving donations, large and small, ever since its creation. For tax reasons all of the money had to be kept in foreign banks until the Peace People could establish themselves as a nonprofit organization. Rumors began to spread that the leaders of the Peace People were keeping the money for themselves. Finally the money became available in March. The first thing the Peace People did was purchase a large building in Belfast for their headquarters. They named it Peace House, and it remains the Peace People's headquarters to this day.

By March, the group had enormous expenses to pay off including travel, phone, and hotel bills. Both Betty and Máiread needed clothes for the numerous functions to which they were now being asked to attend or speak. Neither one of them had the money for a fancy wardrobe. However, as Betty and Máiread began to appear on television and in photographs in expensive-looking clothes, people began to wonder if the two women were using the Peace People's money for themselves. In fact, all of the money the women spent went toward their work for

The Peace People headquarters on Lisburn Road in Belfast.

the Peace People. Betty and Ralph were actually in debt because of their involvement with the peace movement. Still, criticism continued to come from people who did not understand.

In spite of this pressure, Betty, Máiread, and Ciaran received some encouraging news. The number of killings in Northern Ireland had dropped significantly! Whether it was a result of the Peace People or not was still not clear, but they did not care. What mattered was that the violence was decreasing.

The Peace People held their first convention in April. Many topics were discussed including education, trips abroad, and new projects such as youth clubs, community associations, and projects to provide people with work and housing. The Peace People announced that as of March they had received 300,000 signatures on the Declaration of Peace. The petition Betty Williams had started had come a long way. Relations between the peace groups were also discussed and a plan was established for the months ahead.

The three leaders stressed that there was still a great deal of work to be done in bringing about an end to the violence. Máiread asked all of the Peace People to have courage for the work they would be faced with in the days ahead. The Peace People planned to return to the locations of their most successful and significant marches: the River Boyne, Shankill and the Falls Road in Belfast, and Derry.

While Betty and Máiread had said on numerous occassions that they did not align themselves with

A peace gathering on May 29, 1977. Máiread Corrigan (second from right) and Ciaran McKeown (with pipe) leading. There were some rumors at the time that the leaders were spending money that was meant for the peace movement on themselves.

any political party, they were put to the test in August 1977. Elizabeth II, Queen of Great Britain and Northern Ireland, visited Northern Ireland despite threats from the IRA. It was the year of the Silver Jubilee—the twenty-fifth anniversary of the Queen's coronation—and she was visiting her entire kingdom and its former colonies. The police and the British army amassed a huge force of 32,000 to protect the Queen.

Several hundred people were invited to dine with the queen aboard the royal yacht, the *Britannia*, including Máiread and Betty. This presented the two women with quite a dilemma. If they accepted the invitation, they risked losing the support of Catholics who were hostile to the monarchy. Not to accept might appear as if they were against the crown and alienate the Unionists. To complicate matters fur-

Máiread Corrigan (left) and Betty Williams (center) meet Queen Elizabeth during a dinner that stirred up much criticism from Republican and Nationalist supporters.

ther, the dinner was to take place on the first anniversary of the deaths of the Maguire children. They decided they should go and risk people's anger. As expected, many Catholics were angry with their choice and this contributed to a decline of support for the Peace People.

On October 7, 8, and 9, the Peace People held their first assembly in Belfast. The assembly consisted of three days of discussions, work, reports, and voting. The numbers of people active in the peace movement had dropped dramatically over the previous year. Only fifty-one peace groups were in attendance. The decline in membership was understandable. After the emotional high surrounding the rallies during the first phase faded, there was some disillusion with the Peace People as they assumed a lower profile for the second phase of their movement.

The movement's activities were doing well, but some of the delegates spoke out once more about the many trips that Betty, Máiread, and Ciaran took. The trio responded that the trips were necessary to educate people that the war in Northern Ireland was not a war about political liberation or religious difference, but rather about the unequal distribution of political and economic power. They also needed to educate people about their movement and try to gather financial and moral support.

At the assembly, the Peace People agreed that they wanted to introduce another dimension to their work. From now on they were going to concern themselves not only with Northern Ireland but with the whole world. They would ask the people of Northern Ireland to help the inhabitants of other war-torn countries.

All in all the assembly went very well, and on

Monday, October 10, Betty, Máiread, and Ciaran felt satisfied with the Peace People's accomplishments and goals. Betty was in London to receive an award at a "Woman of the Year" luncheon. Máiread was home answering her mail and Ciaran was at Peace House, working on the next issue of *Peace by Peace*.

Suddenly, a number of telephone calls and the arrival of television crews interrupted Ciaran. As Máiread arrived at Peace House for lunch, the media began to ask about the Nobel Peace Prize.

The awarding of the 1976 Peace Prize had been postponed, and apparently the winners were to be announced that day at 3:00 P.M. Betty and Máiread had been nominated too late to receive the award the previous year, but when the Nobel Committee had considered other candidates, none of their accomplishments stood out as strongly as the Peace People's. The committee decided to wait to see if indeed the Peace People would be a lasting force for change or if they would simply fizzle out once the rallies were over. The world was about to learn of their decision.

Some of the journalists speculated that the Peace People might win but Ciaran told them they were wasting their time. Surely he, Betty, and Máiread would have heard something if they were being considered for the prize. But he took Máiread aside and told her that the Nobel Peace Prize might be awarded in some way to the Peace People.

Just after 3:00, Máiread was called to the telephone. She was told that she and Betty had been awarded the 1976 Nobel Peace Prize.

Chapter 7

THE NOBEL PEACE PRIZE AND THE CONTROVERSY

The next day, newspaper headlines throughout the world announced that the 1976 Nobel Peace Prize had been awarded to two women from Northern Ireland. The *New York Times* printed the Nobel Peace Prize Committee's praise for Betty and Máiread for having "paved the way for the strong resistance against violence and misuse of power. . . . Máiread Corrigan and Betty Williams acted from a profound conviction that the individual can make a meaningful contribution to peace through constructive reconciliation."

Betty and Máiread could not believe the news. But they still were not completely happy. Ciaran had been left out. He had not been included because the nominations had been made early on in the movement, when Ciaran was only working in the background.

The three leaders agreed that the prize would be accepted in the name of the Peace People and of all the people of Northern Ireland who wanted peace. When reporters asked Máiread what the prize meant to her she replied, "To me, the Nobel Prize means that we can change the world through nonviolence; and many people will keep that vision before them as I will." Máiread also said that she felt the prize should have gone to many other people.

When the journalists asked her what she would do with her share of the $140,000 prize, she responded jokingly, "My mother always told me that I'd never have any money because I always give it away. Maybe now I can buy that fur coat everyone has always talked about." She was referring to the rumors that had circulated over the past year about her and Betty's fancy clothes. Her attempt at humor would later come back to haunt her when controversy about the prize money arose.

When Betty learned about the prize she was very surprised. She was also exhausted from the hectic pace she had kept over the past year. When reporters inevitably worked their way around to asking about the money, she replied, "Personally, I don't know what to do with [it]. Máiread and I are not going to spend it as many people think. We're going to put it into our trust [the Peace People Trust]." As events

Máiread Corrigan's Nobel Peace Prize medal is exhibited in the Ulster Museum, Belfast.

played out later, however, Betty might have regretted this statement.

Betty also said that the rumor that the Peace People were rich after receiving the Norwegian People's Prize the previous year was untrue. The truth was that the Peace People had several projects underway and funds were still desperately needed.

Soon after the prize was announced, people throughout Northern Ireland began to grumble about Betty and Máiread and "all that money." Even within the Peace People there had been some jealousy about all the attention and opportunities to travel that the women had received. Some people had forgotten what good the Peace People had done and still continued to do.

Máiread and Betty tried not to let these rumors affect them as they prepared for the awards ceremony to be held on December 10 in Oslo, Norway. The Nobel Institute requires that the winners make two speeches, a short "thank you" speech given immediately after the award ceremony and a longer lecture that is given the following day. The Institute also requires a copy of the lecture in advance so that it can be translated and copied. They all agreed that Máiread would give the shorter speech, preferably in Norwegian, and that Betty would deliver the longer address.

Later, Ciaran recalled that as the Institute's deadline approached for a copy of the lecture, he grew concerned because none of them had met to discuss it. Finally, with only a few days left, he sat down to write his own draft of the lecture and arranged to meet with Betty and Máiread to discuss it.

When he arrived at Betty's house, Betty angrily grabbed the draft from him, saying, "I thought the

What is the history of the Nobel Peace Prize?

The Nobel Prizes were established in 1901 by a very wealthy Swedish chemist and inventor named Alfred Nobel. When he died, he left most of his fortune as a fund from which annual prizes would be awarded to those who bestowed by their work "the greatest benefit on mankind." The prizes are awarded for physics, chemistry, physiology or medicine, economics, literature, and peace. They carry a cash award of about $1 million and bring international attention to the recipients' work.

The winner of the Nobel Peace Prize is chosen by the five-member selection committee appointed by Norway's parliament. Candidates are submitted by members in a number of international groups, including past and present members of the Nobel committee or the Norwegian parliament, different countries' national assemblies and governments, the International Courts of Justice and Arbitration, the International Peace Bureau, present university professors of law, political science, history, and philosophy, and past winners of the Nobel Peace Prize.

Once the names of the proposed candidates are submitted, the director of the Nobel Institute puts together a list of personal information about each candidate. (The average number of candidates is about 100.) At another committee meeting more information is required about candidates who have been nominated. It is up to the director and the advisers of the Nobel Institute to gather this material, often with assistance from the Institute's library (which is open to the public). Their findings are then forwarded to the committee members for consideration. After a series of meetings, the committee makes a final decision, usually in the first half of October, and the award is announced soon after. The presentation ceremony is held on December 10, because this date is the anniversary of Alfred Nobel's death. Ceremonies are held both in Stockholm, Sweden, and in Oslo, Norway. Recipients of the Nobel Prizes are known as Nobel laureates.

three of us were going to write this!" Ciaran reminded her of the pressure they were under because of the deadline. When Betty read the lecture she was so moved she began to cry. She loved it and practiced delivering it over and over again.

The awards ceremony proceeded with warmth and dignity and Betty's speech was received enthusiastically. In the speech, Betty told of the tragedy that led them to make that first demand for peace. She described how their first acts had unleashed a flood of desire for peace in the citizens of Northern Ireland. She stated "as far as we are concerned, every single death in the last eight years, and every death in every war that was ever fought represents life needlessly wasted, a mother's labor spurned."

In fact, Betty was the first mother to receive the Nobel Peace Prize. In the seventy-five years since the award had been established there had been only three women laureates. Now Betty declared that she and Máiread felt that women had a special role in the struggle for peace. "The voice of women has a special role and a special soul-force in the struggle for a non-violent world," she said. She encouraged women to persuade men to say no to war, to have the courage to try to break down the barriers that divide people. "The only force which can break down those barriers is the force of love, the force of truth, soul-force."

Finally she spoke of the Peace People's deep and passionate dedication to the cause of nonviolence. "To those who say we are naive, utopian idealists, we say that we are the only realists, and that those who continue to support militarism in our time are supporting the progress toward the total self-destruction of the human race."

Máiread and Betty followed the ceremony with a tour of Norway before returning home to Belfast. Their arrival home was a shock. The Peace People organized a welcoming rally for the women at Belfast's City Hall. Only 2,500 people showed up. They had received one of the most prestigious awards in the world, yet there was no welcoming ceremony other than a hurriedly organized congratula-

How many women have won the Peace Prize?

The first prizes designated in Alfred Nobel's will were for physics, chemistry, physiology or medicine, and literature. But a friend of Nobel's, peace activist Baroness Bertha von Suttner, had drawn his attention to the international movement against war that had been organized in the 1890s. Nobel had given the Baroness financial support for her peace activities. It was her work that influenced his decision to amend his will and add a peace prize to the other five prizes. He died soon after the second will was drawn up.

It seems apparent that by adding the prize for peace, Alfred Nobel thought that the Baroness would receive it. But four other recipients would have the honor before she finally received the prize in 1905. It took another twenty-six years before a second woman, Jane Addams, was given the prize, then fifteen more years until Emily Greene Balch shared the prize with John Mott of the YMCA in 1946. It wasn't until thirty years later that the next women, Betty Williams and Máiread Corrigan, were honored with the peace prize.

Since then the committee has honored Mother Teresa in 1979, Alva Myrdal in 1982, Aung San Suu Kyi in 1991, Rigoberta Menchú in 1992, and Jodi Williams in 1997. Yet of the ninety-seven Peace Prizes awarded since 1901, only ten have gone to women, even though numerous women have been nominated.

tory statement from the mayor's office. Their humiliation continued as they walked down Belfast's main street greeting well-wishers—they had to submit to searches at security barriers in the street. These women, who had struggled so long for peace, were treated as if they might be carrying weapons.

The two women only made the situation worse a few days later, and struck a devastating blow to the Peace People. After continually being hounded by questions about what the women planned to do with the money, Ciaran, Máiread, and Betty decided to sit down and discuss exactly what they would do with it so that they could finally give people a definitive answer.

Máiread Corrigan (left), Ciaran McKeown (center), and Betty Williams (right) receiving the Norwegian People's Peace Prize, a year before being awarded the Nobel Peace Prize.

They all gathered at Betty's house. As Betty crossed the living room to hand Ciaran a cup of coffee, she told Máiread and Ciaran that she was keeping the prize money for herself, that she had to pay for some projects of her own. Máiread protested, but Ciaran could tell that Betty had already made up her mind and could not be talked out of her decision. Máiread was upset and shocked. She had assumed that she and Betty would combine the prize money and put it in the Peace People's trust fund. She felt that keeping the money would damage the movement—and events would prove her right.

Betty's decision placed a great deal of pressure on Máiread. As Ciaran and other members of the Peace People pointed out, if Máiread gave away her half of the prize money, it would make Betty look bad and damage both their relationship and the movement. Máiread was torn. Keeping the money went against her better judgment, but Betty was her friend. She decided to take Ciaran's advice and keep the money, even though she felt it was wrong to do so. It was decided that Máiread and Betty would no longer draw salaries from the Peace People. Instead they would continue on as volunteers and use the prize money to pay their own expenses.

Máiread and Betty had a right to keep the prize money. When Alfred Nobel founded the Peace Prize, he intended that the winners should keep the money so that, free of financial worries, they could work harder for peace. The problem was that Betty had already stated publicly that the money would be donated to the Peace People. Their decision now to keep the money only fueled every dark rumor about them and made many people, including members of the movement, very angry.

The credibility of the Peace People was irreversibly damaged and things only continued to go downhill. The friendship between the three leaders began to disintegrate. Máiread and Betty began to argue and again the issue was money. Contributions to the Peace People dwindled in 1978 and the organization needed money badly. Betty had traveled to what was then West Germany several times and met with members of the government, investors, and financiers about investing in Northern Ireland's economy. She hoped that these people would donate money to the Peace People as well. However, these potential donors did not want to be associated with controversy.

While Betty wanted to court German money for the movement, Máiread wanted to speak out about injustice, particularly the plight of political prisoners—a controversial issue that had become very important in Northern Ireland over the previous year.

The relationship between Ciaran and Betty was also growing sour. Disagreements sprang up in the Peace People executive committee as members argued about finances. People began to take sides, some for Betty, others for Máiread. The movement was dying and Ciaran, Betty, and Máiread were too busy and too tired to see it. Perhaps they could have worked out their differences if they had been able to make more time to be together and work toward some understanding, but both Betty and Máiread's personal lives were in upheaval.

In 1979, Betty's marriage fell apart. The peace movement had taken its toll on her family life, and even though her husband had tried to involve himself as much as he could, Betty's constant trips and the continuous demands on her time put a strain on their marriage. Although Betty had been supportive of him when his career took him from his family for months at a time, there was a double standard in society. Women were expected to stay at home and take care of the family—something Betty could not do as the leader of a peace movement. Also, all of the negative feedback Betty received over keeping the Nobel Prize money only put extra stress on the relationship. Finally, they agreed to separate. Betty blamed herself for their breakup, feeling that her involvement with the Peace People had caused her to neglect her family. In fact, like many women, she had been faced with an impossible choice—a choice between two things, her family and her work, about which she cared deeply.

Meanwhile, Máiread was preoccupied with her sister Anne's troubles. After the accident, Anne recovered physically, but never mentally or emotionally. She moved to New Zealand to try to start over, and she gave birth to a little girl. But her family eventually returned to Belfast.

The doctors said that her brain had been bruised in the accident, leaving Anne in a permanent depression that would never heal. Anne could not stop brooding over the deaths of her children—even after the birth of Joanne and, in 1979, the birth of another daughter, Marie-Louise.

In January 1980, Anne Maguire killed herself. She left a note asking her family to forgive her for what she had done but that she had found "peace" finally, the only way she could. Her death was mourned throughout the world. The tragedy on Finaghy Road four years prior had finally claimed its last victim. Heartbroken by the devastating loss of her sister, Máiread attempted to repair her friendship with Betty and Ciaran, but it was too late.

The next month, Betty resigned from the Peace People. The relationship between the three leaders had become so strained that they could no longer work together. Wanting to avoid further damage to the peace movement, Betty quit. Máiread followed Betty to her house to try to talk about the decision, but Betty was too tired and frustrated to talk. She told Máiread she was leaving. After Máiread walked out of Betty's house that night, it would be eight years before they would see each other again.

Betty left almost immediately for America. She would never live in Ireland again. When word of her resignation hit the news, Máiread was besieged with requests for interviews since no one could reach Betty. There was a great deal of speculation about what caused her to resign and several inaccurate articles were written. Many articles blamed it on the prize money, but in reality the division had more to do with the three leaders' different ideas about how to work for peace.

Ciaran was completely disheartened at the breakdown in the relationship among the three of them. The organization became riddled with internal fighting and bickering. People disagreed over who should be in charge and what type of work the Peace People should be doing. Without the inspiration of Betty and Máiread, many people lost interest in the movement. Ciaran decided he wanted to work on some peace projects of his own, do more writing, and spend more time with his family. There was even some talk of him leaving the country. He too pulled away from the Peace People.

Finally, Máiread also resigned from the organization. Like Ciaran and Betty, she needed to go inward, back into the private life she had neglected for the peace movement. After the heartbreak of broken friendships, arguments, and the death of her sister, she needed some time to heal.

Chapter 8

THE WORK CONTINUES

To Máiread and Betty, it seemed like a lifetime since that fateful day in August 1976, when "The Troubles" claimed the lives of the Maguire children. Since then they had experienced everything from inexpressable loss and suffering to the unbelievable highs of world-wide fame and glory. They had sacrificed a great deal for the peace movement, letting it take over their lives, but now it was time to step back and put their lives in order.

Betty and her children settled in Huntsville, Texas, where she took a job teaching at a university. She loved everything about the United States, especially the sun and beaches of Texas. The strife-torn streets of Belfast seemed very far away.

Still, Betty's desire to work for peace never left her. News of the war in Bosnia and other countries throughout the world reminded her of the violence in Northern Ireland. The effects these conflicts had on the children of these countries made a deep impression on her. She decided to devote her life to helping children in all parts of the world.

While still in Huntsville, she founded the Global Children's Foundation, a nonprofit group dedicated to helping children in crisis areas of the world. She developed a plan to try to persuade nations to adopt policies that would ensure the safety and well-being of children. Betty's friend and fellow Nobel laureate, Archbishop Desmond Tutu, shared Betty's concerns for the children of the world and agreed to become an adviser to the Global Children's Foundation.

Betty found her work very fulfilling, but on a personal level she was lonely. In 1981, she and Ralph were finally divorced. That same year she and the children went on a vacation. On their first day of their vacation, she met a man named James Perkins. James was a civilian worker at nearby Elgin Air Force Base. The two were inseparable from that first day. They were married in 1983.

Betty and James moved to Florida in 1989 and still live there today. Betty devotes her time and energy to the World Centers of Compassion for Children and the Mothers of the Earth for World Peace. These organizations reach around the world in an effort to promote nonviolence and create safe havens for children living in countries ravaged by war. She has many public speaking engagements,

Betty Williams with Hurt and Carol Porter, cofounders of KidCare, Houston, Texas. Betty Williams devoted her time and energy to children's organizations worldwide when she left the Peace People and moved to the United States.

including at the United Nations, where she continues to champion the cause of peace. People who inspire her peace work are fellow Nobel Peace laureate Aung San Suu Kyi, Corazon Aquino of the Phillipines, the Dalai Lama, and Martin Luther King, Jr. As feisty and outspoken as ever, Betty continues to crusade for peace.

Máiread stayed in Belfast. Shortly after the death of her sister Anne, she moved into Jackie's house to look after Mark and the two little girls Anne had left behind. Most people, especially her mother, did not approve of her decision. It seemed improper for a single woman to move into the house of a widower, especially when the widower was her brother-in-law, but Máiread strongly believed it was the right thing to do.

Like Máiread, Jackie was emotionally weary. The past four years had been a real struggle as he tried to cope with the deaths of his children and Anne's depression and suicide. He had been a rock of strength for Máiread and her family after Anne's death, but now as a single father of three he needed support.

It surprised both Máiread and Jackie when they fell in love. While some of her family did not approve, to Máiread it was a miracle. She and Jackie made each other very happy. They were married on September 8, 1981, at the Church of San Silvestro in Rome. An Irish priest conducted the ceremony.

A year and a half later, Máiread found out she was pregnant. John Francis was born in 1982 and was followed by another son named Luke, born in 1984. Máiread and Jackie and the five children moved to a small village outside of Belfast, where they still live. Máiread is a homemaker and volunteer, and Jackie works as a car mechanic. They live simply, but comfortably. Máiread is an admirer of Gandhi and a vegetarian. Her faith still plays an important role in her life. She is still very active in the cause of peace, and she fasts for forty days each summer to promote nonviolence.

Her work against violence brought her to the United States in 1998 to oppose the use of military force against Iraq. It also landed her in jail. She was arrested in Richmond, Virginia, after refusing to leave a federal prison in a show of support for a jailed American peace activist named Philip Berrigan. A federal judge dismissed the charge and freed Máiread.

She has also been quite outspoken about the role of the churches in the Northern Irish conflict. In a recent newspaper column she declared, "What's needed in Ireland—and the Christian world—is that Church leaders and Christians must renounce the Just War Lie." She was referring to the belief that

The Maguire family pose for a family picture in July 1989. From right to left: Jackie, Joanne, Máiread, Mark, John; kneeling in front, Marie-Louise, and Luke.

some wars are justified. All too often, and not only in Northern Ireland, religion is used to justify violence. Máiread continued, "Violence is a lie, violence is not the way of Jesus, violence is not the Christian way." Máiread continues to go down to Peace House as a volunteer to work on a variety of their projects. In 1998 she was named honorary lifetime president of the Peace People. She also travels widely to speak about peace and nonviolence and the conflict that, after thirty years, still grips Northern Ireland.

Although their membership rolls and funding are greatly reduced, the Peace People continue to work for nonviolence, not only in Northern Ireland but throughout the world. For such a small organization, the number of projects they have taken on is quite ambitious. They continue to work with young people, families of prisoners, and community groups of all backgrounds to try and heal the divisions in Northern Ireland. The Peace People coordinate summer camps in Ireland and Europe to bring Protestant and Catholic children together in a peaceful environment. They provide transportation for families who lack other means of transportation to visit relatives who have been imprisoned. As part of their welfare program they provide informal education, advice, and counseling. They also maintain a lobbying effort through a petition for peace, their Citizens Campaign and Campaign for a Gun-Free Northern Ireland, and letter-writing campaigns. They publish the *Citizen* newspaper and sponsor several local community peace groups and "People's Peace" talks.

The Peace People have also focused on the emergency criminal justice procedures imposed by the British government in Northern Ireland. These harsh procedures have been criticized by Amnesty International and other human rights groups. Máiread has cofounded the Committee on the Administration of Justice, a nonsectarian organization that fights for the repeal of the Emergency Laws. The Emergency Laws are the Emergency Provision Act and the Prevention of Terrorism Act which allows law enforcement agents to hold suspects for up to seven days without access to a lawyer or to a telephone. Suspects are also tried without a jury of their peers.

In 1996, Betty, Máiread, and six other Nobel Peace Prize winners helped launch Peace Jam, an international project where Nobel laureates work with high school and college students to organize programs to help make communities safer.

Máiread and Betty were reunited in 1988 when Betty returned to Northern Ireland for a visit. She went to Peace House where she and Máiread sat down and shared memories and discussed the peace work that each was doing on her own. Máiread later told an interviewer from the *Philadelphia Inquirer*, "Betty's my friend. God willing, she will always be my friend. We've been through too much together."

The violence in Northern Ireland continues, although huge steps have been made in addressing the economic and political cause of the conflict. In 1994, the IRA and the Loyalist paramilitaries called a ceasefire. The political parties of Northern Ireland entered negotiations chaired by former U.S. Senator George Mitchell. In April 1998, history was made when all of the political parties endorsed the Northern Ireland Peace Agreement, also called the Good Friday Agreement. The agreement granted greater rights to

Catholics while assuring Unionists that Northern Ireland's ties with England would be maintained. The agreement established a new political assembly to enact reforms to give Northern Ireland's Catholic minority greater political power and set up cross-border bodies of legislation between Northern Ireland and the Republic of Ireland.

In spite of these great strides toward peace, there are individuals filled with hatred and bigotry. July of 1998 saw an increase in violence as the Loyalist Orange Order held its annual marches throughout Northern Ireland. The violence and destruction reached a horrifying low point when three young Catholic brothers, aged ten, nine, and seven years old, burned to death in their bedrooms when Protestants threw a petrol bomb through window of their home. The following month a bomb set by an IRA splinter group calling themselves the Real IRA

Women march with a peace sign reflecting the sentiments of a majority of the residents of Northern Ireland.

A funeral for children killed during violence that erupted while Protestants marched through a Catholic community. During the "Troubles" it seemed no family in Northern Ireland could be unaffected by the violence.

exploded in the town of Omagh, claiming thirty-one lives both Protestant and Catholic. Shortly afterward, the Real IRA called a ceasefire. These tragedies only show how much more work still needs to be done before this troubled land will know peace.

For this reason, the story of Betty and Máiread remains timely and important. They were a secretary and a homemaker who grew up in the working-class district of Belfast without a college education. Yet they went on to mobilize hundreds of thousands of people throughout the world to work toward an end to the violence in Northern Ireland. Betty and Máiread showed just what kind of a difference "ordinary" people can make.

It is impossible to measure the full impact of the movement they founded because the work was about changing people's minds and hearts, a subtle change that happens over time. The fact that they made mistakes as leaders of the Peace People serves only to remind us of their humanity, a fact that was often forgotten in the media frenzy that surrounded them. That they have continued—in spite of their fear, mistakes, and failings—to work for what they know to be right makes them that much more heroic. In the words of Egil Aarvik, vice-chairman of the Nobel Peace Prize committee, "Love of one's neighbor is one of the foundation stones. . . on which our Western civilization is built. . . . It is vital that we should have the courage to sustain this love of our neighbor in the very circumstances when the pressure to abandon it is at its greatest—otherwise it is of little worth. This is why it should shine forth when hatred and revenge threaten to dominate. . . . Betty Williams and Máiread Corrigan have shown us what ordinary people can do to promote the cause of peace."

CHRONOLOGY

1921	The government of Ireland establishes the State of Northern Ireland and the Free State of Ireland.
1943	Betty Williams is born in Andersonstown, Belfast.
1944	Máiread Corrigan is born in the Falls Road section, Belfast.
1948	The Republic of Ireland is established.
1958	Máiread joins the Legion of Mary and volunteers with the organization in her spare time.
1961	Betty marries Ralph Williams.
1968	The civil rights movement in Northern Ireland begins protesting the treatment of Catholics in Northern Ireland. This is the beginning of "The Troubles."
1970	The Provisional IRA is formed. It branches off the Irish Republican Army (IRA), which was founded in 1913. The IRA was originally called the Irish Volunteers.
1972	Bloody Sunday in Derry. As a result of the rioting that ensued, the Unionist government in Northern Ireland is dissolved. Direct rule from the English Parliament is imposed.
August 10, 1976	Máiread's sister Anne Corrigan Maguire is critically injured when Danny Lennon, a suspected IRA sniper, is shot and killed by a British army patrol as he tries to flee in a car. The accident kills Máiread's niece and two of her nephews.
	Betty starts a door-to-door petition in Andersonstown asking people to sign the petition

	if they want peace. Within minutes she has collected 100 signatures.
August 14, 1976	The Finaghy Road demonstration is held.
August 24, 1976	The first Peace People rally is held in Ormeau Park.
October 1976	Stories that the Peace People are pro-British begin to circulate, angering Republican supporters.
October 23, 1976	The Peace People hold the Falls Park march.
November 27, 1976	The Peace People march from Hyde Park to Trafalgar Square in London, England.
November 28, 1976	The Peace People leaders are awarded a special Norwegian People's Peace Prize.
December 5, 1976	The Peace People lead the Boyne, Drogheda rally.
October 8–10, 1977	The Peace People hold their first assembly.
December 10, 1977	Betty Williams and Máiread Corrigan are awarded the 1976 Nobel Peace Prize.
1980	Máiread's sister Anne Maguire dies. Betty and Máiread resign from the Peace People. Betty moves to the United States.
1994	The IRA and Loyalist paramilitary groups call a ceasefire.
1998	All the political parties of Northern Ireland endorse the Northern Ireland Peace Agreement (also called the Good Friday Agreement).

GLOSSARY

civil rights Rights all citizens are entitled to, including freedom of speech and religion, the right to a speedy trial by jury, and equal treatment under the law.

extremist An individual who advocates political measures that often use violence.

home rule Self-government by a state or country.

internment The arrest and detention of individuals for an indefinite period of time without a trial.

Irish Republican Army (IRA) A Republican organization.

Loyalist One who supports the use of military means to maintain Northern Ireland's union with England.

martial law An emergency measure in which the military enforces the law.

Nationalist A supporter of Irish nationalism, which aims to gain Irish independence from England and end partition. Most Nationalists, although not all, are Catholics.

Republican One who supports the use of military means to end England's involvment in Northern Ireland and partition.

Royal Ulster Constabulary (RUC) Northern Ireland's police force.

sectarian Of or relating to a sect or religious denomination.

Ulster Volunteer Force (UVF) A Loyalist paramilitary organization.

Unionist One who wants to maintain Northern Ireland's constitutional link with England. Unionists are usually, but not always, Protestant.

FURTHER READING

Books About the Peace People

Deutsch, Richard. *Máiread Corrigan / Betty Williams*. Woodbury, New York: Barron's Educational Series, Inc., 1977.

McKeown, Ciaran. *The Passion of Peace*. Chester Springs, Penn.: Dufour Editions, Inc., 1986.

Watson, Rhoda. *Along the Road to Peace—15 Years with the Peace People*. Belfast: Peace People Organization Publication, 1991.

Books About Northern Ireland and Ireland

Bardon, Jonathan. *A History of Ulster*. Belfast: Blackstaff Press, 1992.

Foster, R. F. *Modern Ireland 1600–1972*. New York: Penguin, 1988.

Lerner Geography Department Staff, eds. *Northern Ireland in Pictures*. Visual Geography Series. Minneapolis, Minn.: Lerner Publications Company, 1991.

Ranelagh, John O'Beirne. *A Short History of Ireland*. Cambridge: Cambridge University Press, 1983.

Internet Sites

PeaceJam
(http://www.peacejam.org)

Peace People
(http://www.globalgateway.com/peacepeople/)

Women Nobel Prize Laureates
(http://www.almaz.com/nobel/women.html)

World Centers of Compassion for Children
(http://www.compassioncenters.org/)

INDEX

Page numbers in *italics* indicate illustrations